1

\\The Hunt\

\By: Bryan Loya

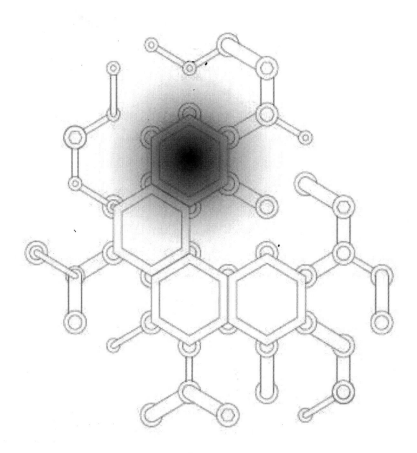

\\Cover by: Bryan Loya and Troy Covington

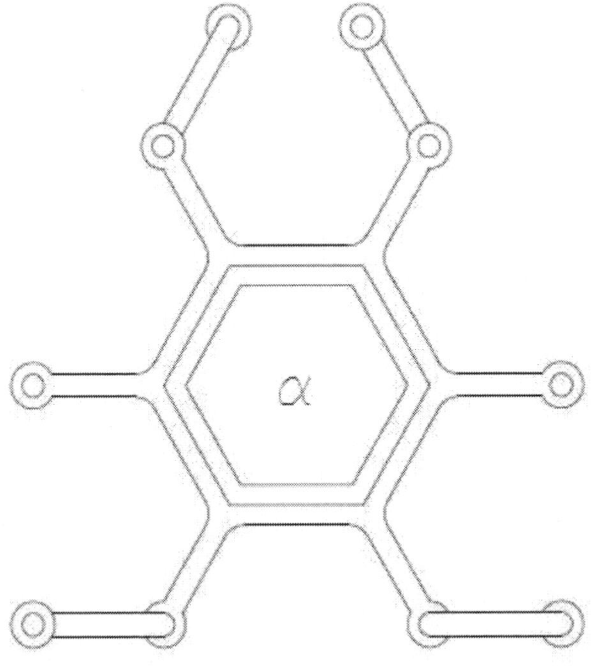
α

Dedication:

Thank you Mom, Dad for supporting me for 8 years of work

Thank you all my friends for putting up with my wild ideas for 8 years, you guys are great.

Thank you my best friend Stephanie for helping me organize my chaotic mind and my stories, the finish wouldn't be so great with your help.

For: Harney Middle School Class of 2007 Las Vegas, NV
Class of 2011 of Las Vegas High School, Las Vegas, NV
Class of 2011 of Chaparral High School, Chaparral, NM

For the future, present and past

\\\\So it begins...\\\

Prologue

August 2002. I was on a bus ride from Lorton, Virginia, when we stopped at the Front Royal Greyhound bus terminal, which was near a train station. All of us, meaning the other kids like me, walked into the train station and we saw a small train being headed by an old steam locomotive. It was black and shining under the station's blaring lights. It had a red stripe running on its side with the number 35 imprinted in the middle of it. Next to it had a brass plate with the letters HPR engraved. The conductors escorted us to the passenger cars that were painted with a glossy maroon coat. The hand rails polished chrome, and the smell, once I boarded the passenger car, was that of a new car smell. Well like a new minivan. As soon as all of us were boarded and the conductor punched our tickets, a man stood in front of the aisle of the first car. I was four seats from him. He pulled his PA microphone. "Thank you for your cooperation," he smiled, "in a couple of hours we will arrive at our destination, Roanoke."

The train whistle blew and we slowly chugged our way out of the station. I looked out of the window and saw a man wrapped with a blanket sitting on a bench, he looked up at me and I we glared for a moment as the train accelerated faster out of the station. I turned and looked ahead at the lavish seats. I was going for real, this is it, there's no turning back now. The train ride was relaxing. Though I wish it was bit more. In the background I kept hearing Cornelius, when I turned around I found out it was just someone's walkman playing the history of the New York Central Railroad, or at least I figure something like that. They said that the train ride to there would change a person especially if you ride this particular train there. Well, they forgot to mention how agonizing it was, or how long it was.

The train rolled through the soothing Shenandoah Valley surrounded by the pristine blue Appalachian Mountains, trees from trackside to the horizon, it was a relaxing scene. I hope it's relaxing at Roanoke. It was nightfall by the time we got the Roanoke Terminal. Well at least at the bridge before the terminal, the Conductor said we were going through Blue Ridge Pass and if I looked ahead out my window I would see the final destination, The Academy. I saw it off to the distance, an old Victorian manor, massive in its size perched on the ridge of what seems to be a rolling green estate with trees high above overlooking what seems to be the rail yard of the north side of the terminal. The yard lights went by slowly as we decelerated into the massive train station. The lights were bright and illuminated the place with such fashion. The train came to a clunky stop. The doors opened and the conductor escorted us out of the passenger cars. We gathered at the platform and looked above the high arched roof, lights, green light posts, walkover that spans all of the platforms. Another man, in a suit with a large grey badge escorted us up the stairs and to the main building (it was massive) with great stone features, so modern looking, I think. The entrance was ahead and it was row of brass frame doors but we took a left through a corridor to another platform but for shuttle buses. "The tram in currently out of order," the man noted, "In turn we will shuttle you via buses up and around the manor access road. Same behavior protocols as tram riding will be applied in the shuttles."

So I boarded these buses, very small bus, and very low too. The convoy began to venture out to the main road leading out of the station and took a turn on a street were we passed a large stone wall with an iron fence on top of it. We saw the front of the man from here, the large glass dome with a garden in front of it perched on the edge of a small cliff. The road was turning slowly but up the hills we saw the back side of the manor, still great but not as the glass dome. The road continued but though a tunnel with blaring white lights. We finally got out of the tunnel and ahead, the grand fountain and roundabout, the road was now brick-laid and the scene was remarkably beautiful. The entrance to the manor was something of a hotel. The front of the manor was illuminated by arc-lamps with the posts painted a satin black, like that steam locomotive. Inside the grand hall was a large stair case leading to a corridor with a large arched skylights. In on the second floor balcony facing the grand hall was a tall thin man. “Welcome to The Academy of Advanced Studies,” he smiled. “My name is Mr. Vanderbilt; I’m the director of the Academy and the Controller of the Old Dominion Historical Railroad Corporation. This Manor will be your new home now under you are of legal age to graduate, here you have everything you wanted and need to successfully become, well scholars, but some of you are here for our M.I.T.-backed engineering program. Whatever it is you are seeking, you will successfully find what you are looking for here and beyond. Now it’s late, I know the train was delayed, so we get onto the room assignments, now, each of you have your own room, this manor has plenty of space for you fellas and the current ones.”

He left through the corridors and I was guided to the residency portion of the manor, I was on the fourth floor, 4031, the man gave me my key and room was enormous. I felt a bit comfortable now; I sat on my bed with my suitcases and backpack on the floor next to me. This really feels like a hotel, that’s I was thinking. Then I heard a knock on the door. It was another man, kinda short, hair not that white with a purple envelope in his hand. “Hi, are you Mr. Loya?” he asked.

“Yes?” I replied shyly, “Who are you.”

"Xaiver Brunel," he smiled. "Director of Engineering, I see you have registered at the academy for engineering classes."

"Yes," I nodded.

"Good, well I have here," he continued and handed me the envelope. "Your classes for this term, the schedule is a bit strange but it our standard in registering classes here, remember this academy is like no other."

"Okay thank you," I nodded.

He left and I closed the door, I opened up the envelope and there was only a piece of paper inside with typewriter ink on it. It read: ACADEMY OF ADVANCE STUDIES ENGINEERING SECTOR NEW TERM REGISTERED COURSES SCHEDULE
STUDENT: LOYA
COURSE(S): 1
COURSE CODE: HPR
TIME: 8:55
ROOM: CLASSROOM 125

It was bizarre. I had one class. I guess it'll be a very in depth engineering class. The next day early in the morning I ate breakfast at the cafeteria and headed my way to room 125, if I can find it. The other personnel of the manor told me it was at the Grand Observation Room, I went there, and the glass dome room had 25 or doors, 125 was to my right I entered it and it was room with large leather seats and desks and a large podium with a big projector screen. The man at the podium was wearing a white coat. "You're here early," the man said.

"Yeah," I nodded shyly.

"Well not to worry, pick a seat and wait until the rest comes," the man chuckled. "In the meantime, just relax."

If I knew what he meant by meantime, by understanding it was alright to come late, I would still be in bed, snoozing away.

I sat in the middle front chair, dozing off, but what I remembered when I was dozing off was thinking about that ragged man at the station, then I remembered I saw him again at the Roanoke station, then I saw the brass plate. The brass plate on the door of this room was the same, then the last thought I remembered before I fell asleep was the train, the steam locomotive, the name of it, Black Bullet. This class was boring. I thought that once I wake up, things will be interesting because I slept in class.

When I did wake up, I was right it got very interesting...

Chapter 1: The Arrival
8/27/03
Late Afternoon

August, the last month of the summer season; people, around this time, are usually packing their things up and started their journey back home where they have to face the harsh reality of Monday land. This also means a massive demand of transportation. Highways, Interstates, surface streets are congested with automobiles. Airports are filled with people and the flight schedules are stretched to their limits. That's where the railroads come in to take the extra load. It was fun to see the trains go by filled with people, in fact I can see them trailing through the Appalachian Mountains. People exchanging at the station down the hill coming in from Virginia Beach, or going there; sometimes I meet and see people from far-off places, the strangest place I heard that was El Paso, not because it's El Paso, but that people from El Paso are here, in Roanoke. Well, if the rails stretched from East to West, you're bound to meet someone from the Western United States, which to me is interesting.

I spend my time, well my free time, watching the trains go by and seeing the busy rail yard beyond the forested hill. I knew I wasn't authorized to go near the rail yard without the upper personnel of the Academy in our presence. Seeing the engineer-in-training fixing and operating the large historic steam locomotives for the passenger operation was amazing, from what I could tell from my three visits to the yard. I usual stayed in the Academy grounds for my studies, and to the old rail yard for some hands on mechanical studies. Every time I'm at the mechanical studies, I usually see the Class J 1950 steam locomotive pulling into the shed for the regular maintenance run. Which I'll be on real soon as the schedule changes, that is usual in the hands of the

Rail yard master. The locomotive was making its way back from the Baltimore yards, they were mumbling about troubles at the Potomac Bridge, some traffic disturbances. I always wondered what it would be like to go there, just at the Potomac River Bridge, to see what the big deal is. Instead I'm here, for a year, in Roanoke Virginia. And by the way, I'm Bryan.

Later that day, some of my classmates, well two in fact came back from their training session on a real locomotive, not the modified Historic steamers, but the modern diesel-electric ones. I asked the one of the Yardmaster's assistants if I could go in the shed for some training, just basic routine cleaning of the equipment. He let me into the yard; I traveled down the trams that lead to a small platform outside the shed. I walked into the small shop area and started to clean parts for the repairs on some of the locomotives. I heard the engineers grunting and pulling off broken steel parts from the engine compartment of the locomotives. I also saw my classmates kissing at the corner of the entrance to the locomotive stalls. They began to walk towards my station where I was loading up some cotter pins, bolts, nuts and the pneumatic wrench. "Need help?" Arthur laughed.

"No, I got this," I grunted.

"Haha, with that strength?" Arthur chuckled. "Whatever!"

He and his squeeze, Martha laughed and walked by, Arthur slapping my back. I almost lost grip of the wrench. I eventually got it onto the flatbed cart. As I was pushing the cart to the engine stalls I was also thinking about how skinny I was compared to him. Then again I'm two years younger than him. I delivered the items to the mechanics in the engine stalls; while I as in there, I noticed they were taking measurements of the Class J locomotive, nicknamed *Black Bullet.* As I gather empty canisters and boxes with oiled rags I went back into the shop section of the shed. I was looking back at the engineers taking measurements of the locomotive; I wasn't looking ahead of course and ran into Sally. She locked on to me with her beady green eyes. "Watch it!" she yelled. "If you do this agai-"

"Hey, hey!" I yelled. "Put down that torque wrench and I'll be more careful."

She didn't really say anything, much like the other times I ran into her around the Academy grounds. She just gave me a "You're dead to me" face, which is worse than the cold shoulder she gave me when I bumped into her when I leaving the Library from my literature class. I didn't look back in fear that she might have turned into something like Medusa, or worse. I mean she's not ugly, just that her environment around her is just feels hostile. I went back to my bench work area where Arthur and Martha just leaving. "You finally got that wrench on to the cart?" Arthur asked.

"Leave him alone he must be tired," Martha chuckled.

And lo, they left the building having no clue where they are going whatsoever. So I was left here, alone with a pile of rags from a month ago stuffed in the dark blue lockers. Next to it was empty soda cans and melted Hershey chocolate bars on the work bench how nice. On the other side of the bench were trashed oil cans and cans of WD-40. If that isn't enough on the cold concrete floor was six, count them, six rotten sandwiches. I think we had enough penicillin, thank you. God, I think this is how my mom felt when I was at home. I casually walked to the over-sized closet and pulled out the sweeper and started to clean the penicillin infested floor. After that task I turned my attention to the bench and cleared all of the trash. Then I hauled every rag, empty canister to the large dumpster behind the shed. I went back inside the shed and steered myself into the main office. In there I grabbed a Gatorade from the cooler and started to drink like hell. David came in from his office on the second floor. “Bad day with the dim wits?” he asked.

David was one of the Yard office trainees; he was one of the classmates who had a direct connection the administration offices. He is usually the one who we go to get the heads up with the new work/training schedules for the Rail Yard and the training sessions in the shops. He is also the one who deals the paperwork for everything for these courses that the Academy administers. “What do you think?” I replied exhausted.

“Yeah,” He chuckled.

“Your right,” I chuckled.

“Uh, tell me if I'm wrong,” he asked. “But, um, are you supposed to be in at six-ish?”

“Normally yes,” I explained calmly, “but the 'dynamic duo' left a mess at the shed.”

“Really?” he gasped casually. “Well I think they'll be beaten over at the Santa Fe shops.”

“Yeah,” I sighed in disappointment.

I paused for a while as David was walking through the double green doors. At that moment I realized something really big, something life changing for me and for the two idiots I work with. I ran through the double doors to catch up with David.

“Wait a minute!” I exclaimed. “What do you mean by 'over at the Santa Fe lines'?”

David turned around and smiled at me. “I'll show you,” he chuckled.

Honestly I have no idea of what's going down. David directed me to the timetable in the office. He pointed at a slot reading 'reserved train arrival: 8:45pm departure: 8:55pm'. “See that slot?” he asked.

“Yeah so?” I replied confused in every direction.

“Do you know why this train is reserved?” he asked again.

“No,” I said.

He pulled out a really thick silver folder with the words 'Transfer Files' in bold print. I just gazed upon it. “Let me show you what I mean,” he said cheerfully.

He grabbed a computer and brought up the transfer files and in that long list were two names I love to see now, Martha and Arthur. “No kidding!” I exclaimed in enjoyment.

“Hope that frown will turn into a smile,” he sighed in satisfaction.

“Yeah, who will be the two replacing them?” I asked curiously.

“Two? Three.” David replied.

“You mean I'll have not two but three new crew mates?” I gasped in surprise.

“That's right,” replied David.

“Oh no, that means I'm...” I paused in shock.

David was grinning and nodding his head slowly. “Chief Engineer?” I whispered in complete awe.

“Yup,” he answered.

“They said I was going be that program, but not this soon.” I gasped.

“Believe it,” cheered David.

“So who are they?” I asked.

David threw in three files. “They say that they are the best at what they do. I want know how good they are and what else they are exceptional at doing.” David said.

“That’s why they placed me as Chief Engineer of this little, um, squad?” I asked.

“I believe so,” David replied.

“But, um, I,” I paused.

“No ‘buts’ Bryan,” David interrupted. “You know why you were given that position. We always knew you were a fish out of water, well more like misplaced, in a foreign environment, but that didn’t stop you from doing what you do at the level you do it at.”

"Okay, first, that's a lot of 'do's'," I stated. "And second thanks."

"Take them back to your room," David added. "Look over the files, but make sure you return them before your first session tomorrow."

"Will do," I agreed.

The first folder I opened up was file belonging to a guy named Devon. He works at Union Pacific as an assistant engineer in training. He applied for a job as a Conductor here. The second file was Adam. His job was Yard Mechanic in training and he applied for assistant engineer. Here I paused for a moment I thought about the third one I know this guy applied a job here as an engineer but still it surprised me. The third file applied for and engineering position at the Academy, but it's a she. I mean I know a lot of girls who are engineers but I never expected of having a female partner working with me in the cab. Her name is Sierra, she is the few girls driving a steam locomotive at her yard. It says here in the file that she drives none other than a Big Boy steam locomotive; well under strict supervision of the actual engineers at the Las Vegas Union Pacific Rail Yard. I was blown off my chair, literally. Finally I will not be working with butt heads anymore! My spirits were lifted to soaring heights. And for once I was happy at work.

I was reading the files over and over and over. Every time I read the files again I find something new like that they never went to engineering school but learn firsthand on how to operate railroad machinery. Yup, this is one of those surprises that never runs out of, uh, well, surprises. And damn I just hit the jackpot. I think things will end up nice and cool after all.

By the time I was finished with the files, the transfer train left ten minutes ago. I went up the oak stairway to the second floor where I found David in his office overlooking the yard. "Hey Dave, finished with the files," I yawned.

"That's all right! Keep them," he replied as he was talking on the phone.

"Okey-dokey," I sighed.

As I checked the files one last time I found their arrival time, 9:10pm of today on platform 5. I checked the iron clock above the main entrance of the yard offices, it read 9:07. I grabbed a messenger bag, stuffed the folders into the bag and ran out the main doors into the main hall. I ran down the wide, vast, long, tan tiled hall that lead to all 36 passenger platforms I ran up the tiled stairs onto the overhead walk and down the stairs to the platform with the bright red five above the crowd of people. The *Silver Express* left the right side of the platform as I arrived. A crowd of people stood there waiting for the next train. I pushed my way through the crowd of commuters. And there was the empty spot, reserved for the new incomers. There at the bench I sat waiting for the new recruits. Two minutes passed like 2 seconds. I looked northward and saw a train coming in slowly. The smoke bellowed out of the smoke stack dramatically. Steam hissed out of the cylinder cocks as it entered the massive station. The large blue mogul passed my view point as it reviles the long blue 8 car train. The train brakes came on and the train slowed down to a stop. The dull thud echoed around the platform. Then I saw Andrew hopped out of the back car and blew his whistle once. All of the doors of the train swung open swiftly. Soon a crowd, no, herd of new recruits came pouring out. I jogged towards Andrew and asked him, "Dude are these all of the new recruits?"

He scoffed, "Of course not! There some more tomorrow or later on."

I dropped my jaw, "No!"

"Believe it or not," he laughed. "There's more coming."

I turned my attention to the direction to the crowd. In front was the monster, Evan Boyle of H. R. I followed the back crowd where I found a girl somewhere around staircase 10 or was it staircase 11? I walked up to her and asked, "Need some help?"

She looked up at me with her blue eyes and light red-ish hair. "Yeah," she responded.

I picked up her bag and walked with her. "Come on." I said. "I'll show you to where to pick up your forms."

We walked all the way to the main office where she picked up her forms faster than anyone in line. Soon we were on our way out of the station until. "Hey! Where you're taking her?" yelled Evan.

"To her room," I responded.

"Fine!" Evan hollered. "I'm watching you!"

"Alright," I nodded.

"What's with him?" she asked.

"He's just stubborn one of the upperclassmen," I noted. "Just stay out of their hair and you'll be fine here."

In no time at all we entered, the tram station that'll takes up to the residential portion of the manor, basically the dorms. The tram climbed the lush hillside covered with grass, gray granite rocks, tall oak trees and some evergreen pines. At the manor's tram stop, we got off and onto the red bricked walkway, the late Victorian era street lamps illuminated the walkway with brilliant white lights. "Different from Las Vegas," she pointed out.

"Really how so?" I asked.

"Bunch of neon lights, just illuminating the sky, you don't see the stars as well until you go the outskirts of the city," she explained.

"Huh, well I'm guessing you lived on the edge of Las Vegas?" I asked.

"Sunrise, the eastern edge of the city," she answered.

"Well you'll feel at home here, we're basically on the edge of the city, the city wraps around these mountains to the east and north and the west. It's like an outpost up on the hill watching the city day and night," I explained. "It's nice up here, trust me."

"It is," she smiled.

We reached the entrance to the dormitories; it looked like the entrance to a ritzy hotel. Inside there was the grand hall that separated the classrooms to the right and the dorms to the left. I lead this girl up the main magnificent staircase to the fourth floor. "What was your number?" I asked for the umpteenth time.

"Room 4033," she said.

I murmured the number. "Oh, you are nowhere near me," I said stupidly.

She laughed. I dropped her bags in her room. Suddenly she asked me, "What's your name again?"

"First name Bryan, yes," I responded. "How did you know?"

"That guy, um, Evan, the one who yelled at you," she stated. "Told us our trainers and it mentioned you when my name was called along with others. He came up to me and showed me a picture of you."

I sighed. "And you waited this long to tell me the realization?"

"Yes," she smiled. "I wanted to get in your head."

I felt a little weird at that moment. The feeling was like someone pouring cold water in your spine, like something came through me. "Well, see you tomorrow," I smiled.

"All right," she replied as I left her room.

And so begins my new job as Chief Engineer of the training program on the academy. Time to teach them the ropes, though I have a feeling it's no ordinary ropes I'll be climbing.

Chapter 2- First Day
8/28/03
Morning

Early in the morning the alarm went off like a horn of a Dash 9. I got ready as usual, went down to the dining hall, picked up something quick to eat and headed off to the yard. Apparently it was raining like cats and dogs at the yard. The tarp of the new M.O.W. shed was going up. I found David at the signal tower. “Where are they?” I asked.

“They are at the Office picking up their work orders.” David replied. “Yours will be there soon.”

“Alrighty then,” I sighed in relief.

I ran to the shed where I found 6 new crews waiting. “Who you are waiting for?” I asked.

A short Asian looking kid turned around and replied, “25.”

“They are at the repair shop picking up the replacement,” I replied.

He just nodded and left. As soon as they left I found her, the girl from yesterday with one short stupid looking guy and another big fellow. I cautiously walked towards them. “Need some help?” I asked to the short stupid one.

“Yeah we are looking for 35.” he coughed.

I didn't know what to say. All I did is just raised my hand and waved. “Right here,” I replied.

“Where?” the short stupid kid asked.

I knew at that moment that he is a wise and an idiotic guy. “Here Sherlock,” I replied sarcastically.

“Oh,” he gasped. “I used to be Sherlock for Halloween.”

“Follow me; the engine is at the repair shop for some polishing.” I commanded.

The three followed me to the repair shop at the end of the slope. I looked back to see their face as they entered the shed. "This is the repair shop," I explained, "every locomotive that needs to be cleaned, repaired, replaced, checked rolls into the shop."

I know they weren't paying attention to me, 'caused they were too busy with the cranes carrying boiler sections, wheel sets, etc. Also they gazed upon the sparks coming off the welder's torch as they begin their early bird shift. We walked down a track with a big black 5 on the concrete between the rails. In front was the engine with a big brown tarp being lifted off the boiler; slowly it reviles the newly polished locomotive. The locomotives surface shined as the yellow orange light reflected off the smooth black surface. "How old is that thing," she asked.

"Somewhat around fifty-three years old," I replied.

"Whoa," she gasped.

"Come on lets show you the works," I declared.

All three hopped onto the cab. As I climbed onto the cab I asked, "Hey you girl, are you sure you can drive this?" I asked.

"Uh, I think," she replied.

She looked at the controls of the "J". She turned around. "Maybe not." she replied.

I chuckled lightly. "I'll show you," I sighed.

I climbed onto the cab and pointed to a black handle with a dull silver rods connecting to it on the cabs roof. "On Express engines like this one the regulator is located on the cab roofs underside like this," I explained as I turned to the firebox. "This box basically the same design like any other steamer. The doors opens up like a butterfly wings and you open with this pedal on the floor. You step on it and shove the coal in. the emergency brake is this rope above you. Pull it and the valves automatically shut down and the cylinder exhaust pipes or the cocks open up. The blower valve is located above the water intake valve, remember, the blower valve is blue and the water intake one is red. The water injection one is yellow only open that when this boiler level gage reaches that red line."

"Okay so which gauges is which? " Sierra asked.

"Okay the red gauge is the boiler water level the blue is the water capacity in the tender. The Black gauge is the steam pressure in the cylinders. The Yellow one is the steam chest pressure or the boiler pressure. Important do not let the needle of this gage reach this limit marked by that red digit. The last one is the speedometer the bronze one. Make sure the train doesn't exceed the limited speed barrier on any line. Got that?"

She nodded as she looked at all the valves and gauges. "That's simple to remember" she said confidently, "But what's with the pipes?"

There's something wouldn't expect from any railroader. "Those pipes carry the steam, water, air supply throughout the whole locomotive." I explained. "That air pipe, the black one, is the air brake for the whole train."

"Yeah and I know how that works." She replied.

"Okay, well we have to wait for our Engineer," I noted.

"Wait what?" Sierra asked.

"We have the main engineer train us, I'm just like the medium," I explained. "It's the Academy's policies with the local railroads and the regulations, something like that I think."

"Okay?" Sierra nodded perplexed.

"All I know is that I get some chances to run these bad boys and you guys too," I noted. "But for now, we're not going on this locomotive yet, we are going to the modern ones, the diesel electrics."

"Hey Bryan, haven't seen you for a while," Mac interrupted.

"Ah, yeah, I had several assignments from the Academy." I replied.

"Who's he?" Sierra asked.

"Oh, this is Mac, he works here as an engineer." I explained, and then turned to Mac. "Mac this is Sierra, Devon, and Adam, my new Academy crew."

"Ah nice to meet you," Mac smiled. "I'm going to be your engineer for this first run. So let's get to that ol' Dash 9."

We followed Mac as he recites the safety regulations that the railroad put for the trainees along with the Academy regulations. I already knew all of them so I phased him out, and kept following him. I was just thinking about some things until I came across something in the stalls. I looked down the doors that lead to the workshop area of the shed, I saw a man in a silhouette angrily discussing something with one of the yard managers in the workshop office. I felt that the silhouette looked at me and I had a cold feeling like the one from last night

But much colder and more of a powerful punch. "Here she is," Mac sighed.

The Dash 9 was recently washed and the black paint with the white and red strip glisten under the shed's bright halogen light bulbs. "Where are we going again Boss?" I asked.

"Blacksburg! We have a fast freight train to pick up at the limits yard." Mac replied.

"Limits yard? Huh, that's not too far that's just a few miles." I murmured to myself.

We all boarded the cab of the Dash 9 and we sat on the seats behind Mac's. The engine roared to life, slowly we rolled out from the stalls and past the large classification yards. With dull thud followed by air hissing from the air brakes, the massive steel diving rods creaked into motion. The headlight came on as the head of the engine creaked out just as the day was transforming into a rainy day. The Dash 9 received the all clear to enter the mainline as we headed to Blacksburg.

The train zoomed down the line. During that time my crew members and I learned each other's names and such, like about themselves etc. Before I knew it, we were there at the small limits yard. The limits yard was nothing but sidings (tracks where freight and passenger cars are stored for later use or pick up) branching out from the mainline. In no time at all, we found our train next to the order office. Slowly the train backed up into the siding and with the ker-thunk of the knuckle coupler. See, the knuckle coupler works like this; If you curl your fingers in ward to make a half fist with both of your hands. Now turn one of your hands so the fingers are on opposite sides. Collide them, lock them and you have yourself an example of how a knuckle coupler works. Anyway, we got the train hooked up with the engine. The signal on the side of the tracks turned green. The engine slowly moved as the wheels slowly came into motion. The train rattled over the switch and it was all downhill from here, literally. The line goes down in elevation as it heads south. The line reaches level ground when it hits Martinsville. The Norfolk route which follows into Richmond then to the harbors. The Greensboro route leads to the Coastal Express Route. Today we are heading to Hampton, 12 miles north of Norfolk. I think in this weather and this speed, we'll reach there in, uh, 6 hours. Apparently I was almost right, 5 hours and 51 minutes, but who's keeping track?

"So," Devon peeped, and looked at me. "You're not from around here are you?"

"No," I replied.

Mac laughed. "Kid, in this Academy of yours *no one* is from these parts. Some remember where, but they usually leave," Mac explained. "No one is from here."

"Where are you from?" Sierra asked.

"The southwest," I replied.

"Anywhere specific in that region?" Adam asked.

"South of what you guys call the Southwest," I replied.

"How long you've been here?" Sierra asked.

"All my life," I replied.

"I don't understand," Adam said stupidly.

Mac laughed again. "You'll be saying that a lot in the Academy," He paused. "Some things don't make sense, but they won't let it be, they give you the tools to figure out things. Creative solutions to be made by an engineer. That's why you kids are here."

"I still don't get it," Adam replied.

"It's going to be a thrill ride for you then," Mac sighed.

Mac was right, you have to have you head up and be aware of things going around you in the Academy. Many don't listen to such advice and they either drop out, and go back to their lives, feeling broken because they left the Academy, or just don't get far in the Academy and stay there until they graduate. But the first reason seems a bit weird since they leave feeling different like they miss something. I know this because a person once left the academy and then returned because they couldn't really function; of course this person was Evan. We reached the docks but not our destination. See the docks today are busy as hell. With locomotives going in and out with empty or loaded trains; a man in a rain suit was waving a red stick on the side of the tracks. "First lesson," Mac smiled, "Safety regulations and techniques."

"Okay," I nodded.

Everyone looked out from the cab side window. "Yard personnel sometimes are out here to inspect the rails in case of any more problems that were due to a wreck," Mac explained.

The man climbed onto the crawling locomotive. “Train 3456 from the Southern rails detected an oil leak on their train, now they are cleaning it up. Another is that an electric broke down on a cross-style switch” the man explained.

“So where do we drop the load?” Mac asked.

The man looked ahead, “I think at the first by pass ahead you can stop and rest.”

“Will do,” Mac nodded, “oh, do you want a ride?”

“Sure! And be careful at the bridge.” he responded.

“Why?” Sierra asked.

“Well, when the storm thundered in early this mornin' a small freighter with a crane crashed in to the pier of the bridge.” Mac explained.

“So we have to go slow on this,” I paused for a while. “Wait a minute, the pier is a 10 foot thick concrete support!”

“'pparently the boat struck it so hard it started to tilt to one side.” Mac added.

The train rounded the bend and crossed the steel bridge with the wrecked boat on the opposite side. The dull creaking soon came clear as the locomotive rolled on top of the bridge. “I don't like this,” I sighed.

“Well deal with it there’s no other way,” Mac replied.

The creaking of the steel beams made me anxious. For every rotation the engine made then bridge creaked four times. I think at that point I felt the tilt of the bay bridge. We were at the quarter mark when the bridge jerked downward. “What the hell is goin' on?” exclaimed Sierra.

“I think she can't hold on any longer!” Mac yelled as he swung on the handle.

“Screw this,” I murmured as I put the throttle (or regulator) forward. The train began to pick up speed as the bridge tilted. Beams began to pull apart. The concrete piers began to crack. "Come on you can do it," I whispered to myself.

Mac was clinging onto the handle repeating "Hope she can make it. Hope she can make it."

On the three-fourths mark the train was running up to 90 mph. And the bridge jerked down another 6 inches. The end of the bridge was coming up really fast. I looked though the window in front of me. "We gonna make it!" I chuckled.

With one enormous effort the train jumped a little as we reach concrete ground. "We made it," sighed Sierra.

"Yeah one problem," Mac interrupted, "the oil spill ahead."

My face suddenly turned from happy to anxious. "Oh no," I murmured.

I poked my head out of the window next to me and found that the red flag was just in front of our faces. "PULL THE ROPE!" I yelled.

"What?" Sierra asked.

"PULL THE DAMN ROPE!" I yelled.

With one yank on the rope, our bodies jerked forward as the train skidded on the oiled rails. Slowly the train decelerated to a stop a yard way from the doghouse (caboose) of the oil wrecked train. "Damn that was close," gasped Sierra.

"Hell right you are," I panted.

Mac was laughing as he clings onto the handle. "You still have in ya!" he laughed.

"Thanks," I chuckled.

Mac waved at the man as he left in a rush to get back to the dock for his duty. While for us we waited 'til the train in front of us left. Soon it did limping..........I think; any who, we reached the dock where two towering cranes were lifting containers off the large freighter. The train rolled underneath the web of steel that kept the crane sky high. We stopped at the loading platform of the warehouse on the dock. A crew of dockworkers scramble into the train and carried out every crate there was in the 7 boxcars we have behind the locomotive. When the last box was carried out; crates and drum barrels were loaded onto the train faster than they emptied it. The horn blew as the last container was lowered from the ship, indicating that we were off to another destination, Richmond.

With every tree that passed by the train got faster, strange because the line from the shorelines to Richmond climbs grades. Maybe is the crew factor that's making the train go faster? I don't know really. We arrived at Richmond early in the afternoon. We saw the remains of the storm over the station. Wet, wet, wet, wet! Puddles of water looked like lakes on the platform. As soon as we stopped the train was half empty (or half full, for those people) when we left. No excitement there not anywhere until we started to climb the mountain grades north of Roanoke. Dark clouds loomed ahead as we switched onto the Blue Ridge Route. The boxcars rattled as the locomotive battle the grades of the Appalachian Mountains. The line climbs up north of Roanoke then descends as it reaches the Potomac Valley. There was the big action occurred. See we were on our way pass the Front Royal switching tower when in the stretched of track that crosses the Potomac came a diesel train on the opposite track (is a triple track throughout these parts). The train headed by a Dash-9 seemed to be speeding for no reason until the view got a bit closer. A hotbox (or an over burnt axle) was burning like Christmas lights on all of the places, on the engines trucks (sets of driving wheels). The signal ahead of me was red so we stopped and backed up away. Then another train on the center track was speeding with a 15 car train of hoppers with bauxite pass right by us. The first train tipped to the center track as the other collided to each other head to head. The cars of the center train folded in a zigzag formation as the other 'random' car freight train telescoped into each other. The two diesel engines exploded as they crashed. Black thick smoke was pouring out of the engines while the fire was burning the diesel fuel on the gravel. It was cool for a while but then it got serious when I realized that this is not like any other job, this requires top notch engineering and responsibility.

We were told by the stationmaster of the Front Royal depot to take the Potomac Route as a detour and then head back onto the Blue Ridge Route when we crossed it at Great Falls Junction. When we reached Harpers Ferry, we stayed there for our lunch. Adam cooked his grilled cheese sandwich near the cab heater while I was eating a burger from Burger King. “Serious, what are you doing here?” Adam asked.

“The Academy is a nice place to be,” I answered.

“I mean, things are so weird, it’s hard to believe all this just happened,” Adam explained, “Something is going on and it’s something big.”

“I don’t follow,” I replied.

“Why? Because it’s too much information?” Adam asked.

“No, I’m getting a bit scared of you know,” I answered.

“Don’t worry about him,” Sierra pointed out. “He get’s paranoid and starts huge conspiracy theories about things around him.”

“Once he thought I was a Canadian Agent trying to implement a *commie* healthcare system,” Devon laughed.

“How did you convince him otherwise?” I queried.

“I punched him,” Devon replied.

“It was a bit unnecessary,” Adam said shyly.

“It was unnecessary for you to put spycams in my food,” Devon pointed.

“You put what?” I asked.

"I didn't think that through," Adam quipped.

"You don't think through things period," Sierra stated.

"So what did you do before coming here to the Academy?" I asked.

"I was at the Western Branch of the Academy," Sierra explained. "Kinda doing the same thing, but I got a chance to work at the yard."

"Here we go," Adam sighed.

"Shut up Adam," Sierra quipped.

"What happened there?" I asked.

"See it was three weeks before I came here," she explained. "I was doing some yard duties when I got into a fight with the stationmaster."

A fight? With a stationmaster? Something is wrong with this girl.......I think. "The stationmaster argued to me about the wrecked wall at the construction yard." she added.

Okay, we are getting somewhere, but not that far. "I already paid for it," she paused then sighed. "I guess he was drunk."

Now everything adds up. Thank god I thought she was trouble ready to explode. And you know I don't like that due to my previous adventure. "Then he went to my dad and ordered that I removed from the program." she sighed in sadness.

Okay now I officially lost (again). Removed from the program? What nutcase program is that? "What program," I asked slowly.

"Crew, the crew," she answered.

I froze, now I understood what she said but not the concept of a program. "Oh," I said.

There was a moment of silence, the crackling of the firebox was behind me and the steam was hissing out of the valves at random times. "So are you finish with your novel?" I asked with smile.

Sierra looked at me annoyed, "Shut up."

She climbed onto the cab grumbling. “What did I say?” I asked to myself.

Adam came out with his lunch burnt along with the pan. “Uh, can I have you sandwich?” he asked.

“I told you it was too hot for your stupid idea,” I sighed.

“Well why you didn't stop me?” he replied.

Damn it! He got me there. “If you say something like that again I'll stuff you inside that heater.” I grumbled.

“Don't worry I already did,” he responded.

He turned around and I saw a black mark on the back of his head. “Idiot,” I mumbled.

Another hour passed by and we were off on our way back home. With the train creaking as it moved southbound on the line. It was night fall when we were at the yard. The light brightly illuminated the yard with the dull yellow glow. Mac was tired, we were too. The train rumbled slowly as it backed up into the bricked shed. The dull “thunk” vibrated throughout the locomotive. The chains rattled to a stop. The whole engine shut down as the headlights turned off. “Okay guys see you at your next session,” Mac replied.

So much for their first day, hope I learn more about them...as if.

Chapter 3- Sally
9/22-23/03
7:46:34 a.m.

My new crew mates learned the ropes of the day to day operation, but there is one thing that they haven't been taught, the inside scoop of the Academy, the people. It has been days since that first session, we just have been doing some Academic work instead. Though there have been problems here and there, and it started with Sally.

Sally is a classmate who well people say that we have equally matched skills. Every time we meet we create problems, ones that don't affect us as much, but it does a number to others around us. I always have a bad feeling at the pit of my stomach along with that crushing feeling in my chest, like someone is sitting on you and slowly suffocating you, when I'm around Sally. She does have temper issues, as well as I, but her outcomes are more severe than mines. It was alright between us, just the usual sneer eye look at each other in the hall. It was calming down between us, it was peaceful. That didn't last too long. It was an explosion of rage.

I began work on some of my mechanical projects when all of a sudden Sally pushed the door opened and yelled, "You're dead!"

That crushing feeling I told you about, well it was the worst feeling now since the feeling ten-folded in a matter of seconds. She stormed towards me, her glowing angry green eyes and dark brown hair in a pony tail swishing side to side like those ridiculously large blade pendulums that the old-timey lame villains had in the old movies and books. She had her hands clenched in a fist, one fist was nothing, and the left one had a crumpled piece of paper. She stopped at my table. She slams the paper down on to the counter. It was the roster for the speeder race, and behind it was a flyer for the seminar on restoration of the Steam Locomotives in every railroad. "You see this?" she snapped.

"Yes I have eyes, I think everyone in here could see this," I paused. "But the question you should of asked is whether I understand what's on that, in that case I would of responded, I bet the person I'm looking at doesn't, hence the question that was asked at first."

"SHUT UP!" she yelled.

She pulled the flyer and held to my face. "This! I heard you made some snide remarks about my work during this seminar," Sally stated.

"Not to the audience," I added confused, "just to some people around me and my buddies."

"Yeah?" she asked. "You told them I just work with junk especially that darn diesel during my sessions."

"Well not exactly," I paused. "Your diesel is kinda in disrepair, compared to the others, especially the ones in your shed."

"You mean the only other one which happens to be a steamer?" she asked.

"Yeah that one especially," I smiled.

"Wipe the smile off," Sally snarled. "Not my fault the diesel locomotive is not working well."

I was reluctant to add a comment, fortunately that only lasted about three seconds. "It kinda was," I stated. "You were working on the hydraulic system when you over tighten the hex nut and busted it along with the pressurized line. Now when ever that locomotive idles or cruises in the yard it sounds like drowning cat meowing."

She slaps down the flyer and shoved the other on in my face. "Is this going to be a new things you show me things?" I asked. "For future reference, don't it with knives, screwdrivers, drills, in fact don't do it with things that are sharp and kill me."

"Ugh, mute the smart-aleck remarks," Sally growled.

"Okay so what's this fairy tale then?" I asked. "Sorry I didn't know I had one left in the chamber."

"Speeder race, you signed up after you made that remark about me," she stated.

"Sally, sorry to break it to you but, I make remarks about you every time, so you have to be more specific," I noted.

"Was that a sarcastic remark?" she asked angrily.

"It's not if you have to ask," I replied.

"Well..." she paused.

"I signed that paper after the seminar," I explained.

"WHY!?" she yelled.

"Because it was there on the bulletin board," I continued. "Everyone did it."

"Well you signed up because you wanted to BEAT me at it," she stated.

"You signed afterwards," I pointed.

"Well," she stuttered.

She paused her face got red, she smack my books of the table and stormed off. "Well, at least she was courteous enough to not smack my project off," I sighed.

I was finished with the project class and as I was heading down the hallways, I meet up with Adam. I told him what happened in the lab. He was just nodding and looking down as he tried not to trip on the cracks, the flat surface of the floor and his laces. Wow, talk about multi-tasking. "I always feel weird around her," Adam replied. "Every time I walk by her in the hall, it's like something is not right."

"Everyone gets that around her," I stated.

"Well, I guess, but I get it a lot, like everywhere, mostly," Adam added.

"Like how?" I asked.

"Well, the only other time was during that session," Adam noted. "And I have a strange feeling that it will happen again somewhere else."

"The session will happen again, Adam," I sighed.

"I know but I mean that feeling I get, something is weird here," Adam protested.

"You're just paranoid," I explained. "Sierra told me about it."

"See what I mean!" Adam sighed.

"You really need to see the nurse," I stated.

"Yeah," Adam sulked. "They all said the same."

"What do they say to you in the doctor's office?" I asked.

"Next time duck when you see a wrench fly at you," Adam replied shyly.

"Oh," I sighed. "Sorry to hear that."

"You should hear the ringing I get in my ear," Adam added. "It's horrible."

As I walked down with Adam into the grand hall of the manor and the academic compound, we ran into Sally. "Oh I got the feeling Adam," I shivered.

"I do, but I'm guessing that's the bean burrito instead," Adam groan.

"Hello boys," Sally smiled.

"This is not good," I whispered.

"Hey Sally," Adam smiled shyly.

"Shut up, dork," Sally snapped.

"Okey dokey," Adam replied cheaply.

"So, instead of the official race, where we can settle some competition, how about a one on one race?" Sally suggested.

"Okay?" I asked. "I think I have to refuse."

"Chicken?" she laughed. "It'll good for your personal gain, I mean with all the perfect scheduled sessions and perks and open time in the shed."

"What are the conditions?" I sighed.

"If you win, you keep the scheduled session if not, I do and you have to stay low for a month,' she explained.

"That's seems fair," I shrugged.

"But if I win, well I get your money, your girl and everything you own," she growled.

"Okay dude, your way off." I said.

"Deal or no deal?" she asked.

"Where is this?" I asked.

She smiled cheekily. "The Ol' Chestnut Mine."

That night I felt somewhat afraid. The old Chestnut Mine is known for disasters when it first open. The portal of the tunnel collapsed on the first day. And always the machinery will die when it enters the mine. Something is not right about that, something is not even right about this.

-9/23/03-

The next morning came like a bat flying through the air and hitting your head in bed. I had to get up early in the morning like around two. I found Sally waiting behind the warehouse at the outskirts of the yard, and there stood the mine underneath the mainline bridge. And there it was the two narrow-gauge tracks leading into the dark tunnel. "You got to be crazy," I replied.

"A deal is a deal," she spiked.

"Fine where's the engines?" I asked.

She pointed to two small rusty diesel engines. "Speeders?" I replied.

"Yeah," she replied.

"You know those are prohibited in here," I exclaimed.

"That's the point of the game," she responded, "going beyond the limits."

I stared at the engine then the mine. "Fine," I sighed, "let's get this race going."

Soon we were at starting positions. The atmosphere was tenser than the Bull Run Race. The cold mountain wind blew around the entrance making the century old wooden supports creak like an old man's back on a Sunday morning. Suddenly without any notice, Sally's speeder backfire and zipped ahead of me. I was left in the dust, literally. The speeder finally started and my head jerked back. My neck cracked as the small rail vehicle rumbled into the mine. The wimpy headlight only illuminated the tunnel so little, that I couldn't tell difference if its pitch black or that the headlight is actually working. Then again I wouldn't need that dim bulb, I could feel the sharp curves going left and right, left and right and so on. Finally I think I caught up to Sally, I think. How I can tell? Well I felt something whacked me on my face. I figure that was Sally with her trusty titanium bat. Up a head I saw a dim light the size of a Lego piece.

'The end! The end! The end! ' I thought. *'I'm going to win! I'm going to win! I'm gonna win!'*

For some weird stupid reason, I thought that this was all too easy, way too easy. The portal came up really fast, and then......................I don't know the rest. I think I won, maybe. I thought that because she hasn't picked on me after that. All I could remember from that race is this, I found myself still in the speeder with the front submerged in dirt, shrubs, weeds, etc. Wow. I think I have to set this one out. I need a day off. But strangely thing were changing after that race, peace was all over the yard. Eerie. Yeah I know. Where the hell is all the fights? Where are all the guys in the first aid room? Something is going down in this yard and I don't like it. Whoa there's something I wouldn't say in my life time (I think that's millions of years, I don't know, maybe). All I could say is I'm clueless. I'm completely hoodwinked. I , well, that's enough for today. I'm weary and I just want to go to sleep. Maybe I'll rest on it. Oh yeah, one more thing, I need to visit a chiropractor in, uh, two weeks?

-9/24/03- 8:35:03

Something big and bad is going down. I know 'cause I could smell it or is that just me? Anyway I was confused when I got down to the dark red-bricked repair shop. Business seems to be normal, until I noticed something strange. The oil barrels were gone. I know to you seems like I'm going berserk, but the welders and the mechanics never, never remove the oil barrels from the shop. “Hell, where are the barrels?” I exclaimed.

“They got rid of them.” replied James.

“For what?” I asked.

James just shrugged. Finally I found my crew at the open sided shed next to the repair shop. There I saw no equipment. Nothing. Nada. Zip! “Guys?” I exclaimed puzzled as ever, “Where the hell is all the equipment?”

“What do you mean?” asked Sierra.

“Yeah, you told us to get rid of them!” Devon shouted.

I froze at that moment. Uh-oh, Sally must have told them to get rid of them. “Yeah, I thought you were dead!” yelled Adam.

“Wha?” I paused. “Why?”

“We didn’t see you for a day,” Adam replied.

“Well if we didn’t you see for day, will it be alright for us to think you were dead and pack up your things?” I asked.

“Actually we would celebrate until we found out he’s not dead,” Devon interjected.

“Ditto,” Sierra nodded.

“Damn Sally,” I whispered.

“Oh...” Adam gasped. “This is all Sally’s doing.”

“Wha? How do you hear me?” I asked.

“After being hit by the wrench near the ear and that ringing I told you the other day, I developed super hearing,” Adam explained.

"Okay, why can't hear them?" I asked.

"I don't understand them, they speak in some sort of tongues or something," Adam added.

I looked at Devon and Sierra. "Pig latin," Sierra said.

"See tongues!" Adam pointed.

"Yeah Sally does these things a lot," I pointed out.

"Why?" Devon asked.

"I don't know I mean it's been like this since my day one here at the Academy," I explained. "We always were at each other throats academically and in a engineering aspect as well. You know I thought it was just a jealousy thing or just competition but now with the recent events she has been more on the edge. She always has been trying to push me down especially since I got this position. Now, she's I don't know how to describe it."

"Weird," Adam added, "told you."

"Yeah, she's getting weird and for something, lately she's been at the project labs more often, but in the bigger labs, something big is going on with her and I think it affects the Academy."

"That's a fact?" Sierra asked.

"No, just a feeling, that weird feeling," I sighed. "Well we have worked to do, get the equipment back before our next classes."

Chapter 4- Hazardous Accident
9/25/03
4:25:19 p.m.

Thunder echoed in the saturated air. Rain pounded upon the steel surface of the shed. The raindrops rolled down the roof and rolled down the large windows. The sky was dark with sudden flashes of battery blue lightning. Slow freight trains thundered along the mainline. While for my crew, well we were in the shed polishing the locomotive. The sound of the buffer echoed in the immense shed. Adam turned off this buffer and gazed upon the black surface. "Hey!" he yelled. "I could see my face!"

"Yep," I replied, "that means your finish with that spot, go to another."

He started to buff the front of the engine. All of a sudden Sierra asked, "Does this engine have a name other that 35?"

"Yeah," I replied enthusiastically, "it's *Black Bullet*."

She just nodded, "*Black Bullet*?"

"Yeah," I paused, "you have a problem with that?"

"Nah," she stated.

Then out of the blue a distant explosion echoed in the wet air. "Whoa, was that a lightning bolt?" Devon heaved.

"No," I paused in shock, "it was a crash."

"Where?" Sierra asked.

"From the sound of it, at the junction up south," I responded.

"You mean from the junction yard in the valley?" Adam inquired.

"The one just up here?" Devon added.

"That one?" Sierra gulped.

"God damn it, Yes!" I yelled.

"Calm down dude!" Adam replied.

Then David came in panting and soaking wet, "Guys we have an emergency!"

"We know," I replied.

"Oh, okay things are going be shut down this is serious."

"Wha?" I replied. "You mean is not from the junction at the valley."

"No." David gasped as he ran back to the office.

"Okay gang we need to go now!" I declared.

"Okay," Sierra agreed. "To where?"

"The scene, were going to watch," I replied.

We rushed out and traveled to the yard and then headed to the station. We raced down to the platforms and reached the south yard and grabbed onto a tram that lead M.o.W personnel down to the crossings in the middle of the city. A diesel engine coupled to the large, heavy steel and iron cranes. Crew 24 climbed on to the second train behind the cranes. The wheels slipped then gripped the silver ribbons and the cranes slowly creaked as the train headed out into the cold rain. The sound of the shoveling was drowned by the steam hissing out of the pistons and the sander. The cab was enclosed with a small bunker in the back for the coal. The cab was heated up in no time. We passed various express trains like the *Boston Flyer*. We reached Chaffer's Crossing in record time. The scene was twisted, literally. Empty oil cans (tank cars) telescoped into each other also boxcars, gondolas and mail cars. In front of the train was Two diesels facing the in the same direction compacted. The fire was burning like the wildfires of the barren west. Adding to the wreckage was another train on the crossing. A GS-4 with 4 boxcars wrapped around the Water pipe; on the other line was another breakdown crew already at work clearing the wreck. "This is gonna cost all of us," an M.o.W. worker uttered.

The M.O.W. Guys took control of the crane and started to lift sheets of metal of the track. This wreck kind of reminded me of another aching one I saw over the news. If I recalled it was a Thursday morning in December. I was at the home when a news segment came on reporting a train wreck at Altoona. It said that two locomotives a diesel and an electric crashed into each other on a crossing. The electric was carrying lumber loads to Waynesboro while the diesel was carrying oil loads to Harpers Ferry. I remember the scene of the accident; twisted metal surrounded the folded freight cars, the engines all contorted and what not. The thick black smoke from the burning diesel fuel poured into the sky. The overhead wires fell to the ground and short circuited the whole Altoona Station area. Sadly the engineer of the Waynesboro train didn't survive the crash. The other engineer was pulled out of the blazing diesel engine and rushed to the nearest hospital down the road. The wreck caused a ripple effect to all of the surrounding stations. Arrivals were slower because trains needed to take a detour or slow down in order to pass the junction.

Thankfully the crash here at home didn't take any lives but it sure did take a lot out of both the surrounding railroads. But on the bright side the crash occurred on the bypass of the mainline. The cranes were at work rumbling as they hauled the totaled diesels out of the way. Soon we left the M.O.W. guys with their heavy duty cranes at the site as we headed back to the yard to begin our shift. The engines roared as they headed back up the grade; rumbled through the station then onto the saturated yard.

"I guess your feeling was just about the crash," Sierra noted while we were riding in the tram.

"Maybe," I noted. "I'm, well I guess I'm a bit paranoid now, too much to actually think logically."

"Perhaps yeah," she agreed. "Adam just got to ya."

"He does that huh?" I asked.

"Yeah," she paused. "But recently he's been doing it more, strange."

"Yeah, so we don't have sessions nor classes tomorrow," I stated. "As crew chief, how about taking a ride on one of the trains?"

"We can do that?" Sierra asked.

"Yeah, free pass from the Academy," I smiled. "It'll take the paranoia out of our minds."

A team of two small red switcher locomotives with dingy yellow number plates came chugging through the water stands with a long, 20 coach, silver train with platinum nameplates on the sides of the coaches. That was the *Platinum Express* ladies and gentlemen, a long, slender, lively, attractive, flashy silver train. The train contains four elegant dining cars named: "*Cornelius Vanderbilt*", "*Andrew Carnegie*", "*John D. Rockefeller*" and the "*Collis Huntington*". Along with the four dining cars are two kitchen cars, four baggage cars and four vista dome cars, five regular coaches and one observation car.

The train came to a halt as it stopped under the lights of the station. The *Platinum Express* sparkled in the light of the station. The glassy surface of the train caught the attention of the passengers. The windows of the train gleamed as the passengers loaded the train. Slowly the J coupled with the baggage car with one loud dull thump. Adam rushed down and hooked up the air brake hose. The air hissed as the hose was connected. The air gauge needle rose as the brakes were deployed. Devon ran to the first baggage car as the train was ready to go. I slipped on the rough gloves onto my hands as Sierra shoved coal into the burning firebox. The atmosphere was exceedingly tense, but exciting. Up above the track the circular signal changed from a strawberry color to an emerald color. The fresh air was flushed out with the mix aroma of leather suitcases, burning coal and oil. I gripped the stiff throttle, pushed it 40 percent open, just in case of some heavy traffic down the track. With a dull thump, the driving rods faintly creaked into action. The constant laughing, bellowing, chattering was drained when the earsplitting of the whistle echoed in the thick station air. The long, heavy, train crawled out of the station and into the cold bitter storm. The train picked up speed when we reached the one mile mark. I poked my head out the window where the freezing raindrops bombarded my goggles not to mention my skin. I gazed back and noticed that the yard was nowhere to be seen. We were officially in the northern cut of the valley. The engine rumbled across the steel trestle as it reached a speed of 80 miles per hour. The line soon took a turn to the left as it began to climb the mountainous crane. With this engine, the climb was easy as pie. The locomotive sustained an average speed of 75 miles per hour up these hills. Kind of impressive, when you consider the weight its hauling, that's a thousand tons guys. So in comparison that's a thousand cars up a 3 percent grade, during a rainy season. A marvel this locomotive is! As for us we took our place in front of the train, well the first passenger car.

In less than an hour we were in the forest of the Blue Ridge Mountains. Hundreds of turquoise pine trees whisked by on the track side. It was peaceful when you ignore the roaring engines, the constant rhythmic clack of the wheels on the rails and the rattling of the couplers. Up ahead was the dip, when the line finally declines to the Potomac River. The train was already going 90 miles per hour when we reached the dip. We were beginning to reach a passenger station at Waynesboro, a nice community in the Virginian Appalachian. The trains stopped and we got off onto the large platform of the rustic clapboard depot. "Where are we?" asked Sierra.

"Waynesboro, it's just a stop along the line to Harper's Ferry and Front Royal," I explained. "It's a nice place."

"Yeah, you can see the mountains from here," Sierra noted.

We looked at the foggy Blue Mountains across the tracks, stretching to the other side of the valley. We hung out around the depot; we sat on a bench near the Stationmaster's office where I overheard some sort of situation. "What are they talking about in there?" Sierra asked. "I don't know," I paused. "Some sort of situation, a breakdown."

"Of what?" Sierra queried.

"Um, must be a locomotive stranded on the main lines, they are talking about diverting traffic and sending a crew to haul it to the yards here," I reported. "That's all I got."

We heard two diesel locomotives rumbling past the passing line of the station yard and they headed north. The fumes left a train as they disappeared into the northern horizon. "That was quick," I stated.

"We saw there some commotion in the station as they tried to get trains north from the alleged dead train, to come to the station in order to avoid major delays. "Our train back home should be here," I stated.

"Are you sure?" Sierra asked.

I walked up the ticket teller. "Excuse me when is the next passenger train to Roanoke?" I asked.

"The train should arrive here in forty minutes," the teller answered. "They just passed the dead freight train."

"Thank you," I nodded.

Sierra and I went to the open platform and watched the northern horizon where the tracks lead. "Do these things usually happen?" Sierra asked.

"I don't know," I replied. "This is the first time I heard of a situation like so."

Apparently the people in the Waynesboro Yard, never heard of a situation like so. I heard some yard mechanics talking about rumors about the FBI, and police heading to the site. "What's with all the commotion?" Sierra asked.

"I don't know," I sighed. "Something bad is happening."

"Maybe something bad already happened," Sierra suggested.

"If so, then why is it taking so long?" I asked.

"Well, I heard it's a freight train with some sort of special load," Sierra added. "I heard the same thing about those loads at the Yard back home, but they don't really talk about it much in front of us."

"What you heard?" I asked.

"It's for some projects, very high level, outside the Academy," Sierra paused. "Also some people were arguing about them."

"Where?" I asked.

"The Administration Building," Sierra answered.

"Wh-Why were you there?" I asked surprised.

"I got into a fight with someone at the Yard Training," Sierra explained.

"Oh, I'm going to hear about it tomorrow," I sighed. "The downsides of being Crew Chief."

The passenger train home arrived at the southbound platform. Sierra and I climbed the stairs and started to walk in the covered overpass. I kept looking to the north and I heard a faint boom from that same direction. "You heard that?" I asked.

Sierra was about to answer when a Yard Master ran past us, yelling into his radio. "We've got a problem! Send out the repair and rescue crew NOW!"

"Something bad just happened," Sierra gasped.

"I think it was happening all along," I sighed quietly.

"What's over there anyway?" Sierra asked.

"I think the Wayneboro Campus of The Academy," I paused. "I don't know what they do there, some say it's some sort of high level top secret Campus, but I think it's just an Administration building for this Region."

"It must be important," Sierra pointed.

"Why is that?" I asked.

"That," Sierra pointed to the sky.

I saw six black and white helicopters rushed to the direction of the smoke from the north. "Looks like they are going near the Administration Building," I explained. "Something important must be there."

Sierra and I continued our way back to the train and for most of the train ride home, it was silent, most of the people on the train didn't see what we say, or they did but disregard it. "What's there?" Sierra asked.

"From what I know, it's just an Administration building, some adults there working to keep this Academy program going," I explained. "Nothing else."

"Since it's related to the Academy," Sierra paused. "Are we going to hear anything about it tomorrow during our classes?"

"Doubt it," I said, "Something this disastrous and far away from the Roanoke Campus, we won't hear much."

"Doesn't that seem strange to you?" She asked.

"It does," I nodded, "I ignore it."

"How many strange things have you seen or heard when you were here?" Sierra asked.

"A lot," I answered. "Ever since the beginning, I knew this place was strange and it grows stranger the longer you stay."

"Does anyone know why?" Sierra persisted.

"Listen you're just paranoid, everyone gets that when you're in the Academy," I said.

"Who told you that?" she asked.

"The recruiter," I sighed.

"His name?" Sierra asked.

I sat there silently, I didn't know the answer. "Who was you're recruiter?" I asked.

Sierra gave me a blank expression. "I," she paused. "I don't know her name."

"Strange," I whispered.

"You see my point now?" Sierra pointed.

Chapter 5- Guide
9/26/03
Afternoon

The troubles from yesterday are posted all across the media links in the country. I was on the computer in the lab, surfing the net when I came across a news article. It was saying, "Yesterday afternoon an explosion rumbled the town of Waynesboro. No injuries or deaths were counted. But all rail traffic was halted as the bridge was demolished. Locals are complaining to Old Dominion Railroad for all the trouble they caused."

I shut of the computer and went to the main lobby of the dormitories. No one was talking about that, but the professors from the Science courses were terribly chatty, but it was a quiet chatter when I passed them in the Grand Hall. There were some security guards at the end of the hall where the Observation dome was at. On the electronic bulletin board at the end of the grand lobby where the hallway to the dome began there was a series of canceled classes, two caught my attention: COURSE CODE: HPR ALL CLASSES CANCELED. The next three lines was the other ALL BEGINNER LEVEL YARD SESSIONS CANCELED. "Looks like a short day," I sighed.

Oh I wished I retracted that statement. After my regular classes, I thought I would relax most of the day, but that wasn't the case right after my last class. "Whatcha doing now?" Adam asked.

"Huh? What?" I asked in surprised.

Adam was just standing there next the classroom door. "Adam there is nothing more," I said. "I didn't get any orders or drill papers from David today. Haven't you heard that those courses have been canceled?"

"Yes," He paused. "No, not really, but still."

"Look Adam," I sighed. "Go back to your room, or do something relaxing, right now The Academy and the railroad are acting strange and it's better for us to not get involved."

"I thought they acted strange in the first place," Adam stated. "In that case, I think it's time for us to do some digging."

"Adam," I sighed.

"I mean at the library first," Adam persisted. "And we are not going to go after the info first."

"Why is that?" I asked.

"We need some sort of direction first," Adam explained. "There's too much noise going on. So you have any ideas of where we should look first?"

I began to think way back to when I was on my way to The Academy; I kept hearing the name Cornelius. And throughout my first semester in the Academy, I kept hearing that name too until I gave up the search for who that person was. "Adam," I paused. "Have you heard something strange since you got here?"

"You mean everything?" he asked puzzled.

"No, I mean something specific," I specified. "A name."

"No, just noise," Adam replied. "Where is this headed?"

"The direction you're going to take," I replied.

"And that would be?" Adam asked suspiciously.

"Cornelius," I answered.

"Why that name?" Adam asked.

"I kept hearing it near the administration people and the Academy Directors," I explained. "That was during my first semester."

"Okay do you still hear the name?" Adam asked.

"No, not ever since I stopped looking," I sighed.

"To the library then!" Adam smiled in joy.

I think his disregard for everything else or just the essential context of the conversation just will be the end of me. Then again who is to blame for actions? Well me since I opened my mouth in the first place and caused this chain reaction. Adam was cheerfully walking towards the end of the hall until I called him, “Adam, the library is this way,” I called out.

He turn around, no word, just with the usual dorky face he has walking briskly past me. “So it begins,” I sighed.

I had a strange feeling that it didn’t begin, but yet something started. We walked into the library’s entrance. The large wooden double doors were open and in front of us was the open area with the desks in a grid pattern. To the left were the rows and rows of shelves with books, manuals, novels and other media stuff. To the right of the open space were the large three sided counters, not enclosed the backside was wide open. “Where are going to search for that thing you said?” Adam asked.

“Huh,” I paused. “I thought you were the one with a plan. I just came along to help.”

“Um,” Adam said, “I need help then.”

“Okay,” I sighed. “Well, the Cornelius is name, so let’s look up at the administration index from one the computers. Of course we as students don’t have clearance to access that.”

“Thankfully I can hack,” Adam interjected. “I hacked the system before to get me classes in the afternoon.”

“Wow, is that the only thing you can do without looking like a dork?” I asked.

“Yes,” Adam smiled. “Where are the computers?”

I pointed to the left. “They are past the shelves in the rooms in the back,” I explained.

We walked down between the tall shelves of the library. The books spines were all in an assorted colors but dulled and seemed to be covered with some sort of dust. We saw the computers labs in the back, three black doors each individual labs. Adam didn’t pick either one, he went to the other black door to the side.

That was strange. He was headed to the one in front, the first black lab door but he took a sharp right turn and headed to the black door that seemed to be at the edge of the illumination. "That works too," I sighed.

"What's here?" Adam asked.

"Computers," I replied dryly.

"No I mean this door said 'Computer Lab'," Adam noted. "But it seems too small and not the standard format as the other labs there."

"Maybe it's not used as much as the others," I said.

"Perfect, nobody will interrupt us while I hack," Adam smiled.

"Okay good," I nodded.

We entered the poorly lit room; the computers were off, cold. Adam made himself very comfortable and booted up the computer. The home screen was up and Adam changed it into a black screen with several windows with white outlines. He began tunneling into the computer. More windows popped up, he kept typing away, and he was focused, fixed to the screen. Then he entered some windows that were red, not a fire engine red, but more of a soft glassy red. "Got in," he smiled. "We are in."

"Okay good," I sighed. "Where exactly are we?"

"Don't know," Adam replied. "It's some sort of network, with an extensive indexing computer linked to it. Everyone is on here, but only few have access to it."

"Will we find what we are looking for?" I asked.

"It should take a few minutes," Adam explained. "The indexing on this network is ridiculously fast."

I sat down next to Adam and waited for the results. He was typing away. I thought I had to doze off before I got the results, but in a matter of seconds after I sat down, he got the results. "Cornelius," Adam sighed. "Couldn't come up with a last name, and well there is only one in the index."

"What does it say?" I asked.

"He built this Academy," Adam replied. "Nothing else."

"Well I know these buildings were built in the late 1800's, before the turn of the century, so it must be a Cornelius then," I suggested.

"No, This Cornelius, can't find birth records, it just says he founded this Academy ten years ago," Adam added. "Nothing about the late 1800's."

"It gets stranger," I said.

"Yeah and now it's getting stranger," Adam pointed. "The system shut me out."

"How?" I asked.

"It just did," he sighed. "Quickly, and humanly too."

"Okay you're just getting weird," I sighed. "At least we got some info."

"How does the information we got will help us further?" Adam asked.

"It involves the Administration," I explained.

"So we hack in again?" Adam asked.

"No, in the Administration Building down in the yard," I replied.

"Right now?" Adam asked.

"No, we have to plan this," I explained. "But for now, on your spare time try to hack in from your own computer, do some spying for now."

"Okay," Adam nodded.

"Good," I mumbled.

We left the lab and Adam went on his merry way, out the library, while I lingered around the library around the shelves, then I met up with Sally. "What were you doing?" Sally quipped.

"Um," I paused. "None of your business, no details is needed."

"You're not going to find what you are looking for there," Sally protested.

"Who said I was looking something?" I asked.

"No one but you," Sally replied.

I looked at her blankly with a sigh of frustration. "You are going to snitch?" I asked.

"No," Sally pointed. "There's no point in doing so."

"Then what are you going to do?" I asked.

Sally smiled and leaned on the shelf, resting her side on it. "You know how I knew you were looking for something?" Sally asked.

"Amuse me," I said dryly.

"Simple, we're in the library," Sally laughed. "And knowing you, with our 'friendly' competition, you know a lot of things off the bat, hence why you are in this academy, but you don't know everything, so what it's the natural thing for a person like you to do?"

I stood there quietly, just gave her a shrug. "You go where the information is," Sally added. "But you look where you think the information would be, remember information is not only collected in a library like this."

"Why are you doing this?" I asked.

"If you kept doing what you did, without my genius guide," she paused. "I won't have a worthy opponent, and my purpose will be useless."

"I suspect you are up to something," I interrogated.

"That's a good start!" Sally called out as she walked away. "Everyone has motive, everyone is hunting for something."

"Hunting for what?" I asked.

"No one knows until they find it," Sally explained. "I'm competing against you in this, there are too much uncertainties about this game."

She left the library; I stood there in between the two large book shelves. "So I'm not looking in the right place," I sighed. "Why would I trust her?"

I sighed heavily, walked down the shelves and out the library. The late afternoon light poured out from the high windows of the Grand Hall. "If the library doesn't have what I need," I thought to myself. "Where could I find info on Cornelius?"

I looked down the Grand Hall, towards the entrance; I walked to the main lobby and headed to the windows to the western side of the building. The late afternoon sun was warming, breaking through the pines at the distance ridge. I could see the rail yard from here and the restored red bricked Victorian buildings next to the station. It was the administration building, the main building that administers the rail yard operations and the Academy Operations here at the manor. I saw a group of people leaving the north side of the building and headed to the tram station that'll lead back to the manor. The top guys of the class were coming back from their administrative classes. I thought, well if Adam hacked into the Administrative system to find what we are looking for, which we partly did, and then those guys are much closer to the source. But that advice Sally was nagging me, it was somewhat fogging up my judgment. I mean what if I asked one of the guys who attend those classes to find more info on the subject, and they came up with the same thing. Of course that is if I consider what Sally said about looking at the wrong place. Starting some sort of guide to find out what's going here seems so daunting of a task. Let's look at this way, me and Adam were looking for info on Cornelius, the reason being is that I kept hearing the name since I got here and I heard the name every time I thought that something is off about the Academy. So we thought in finding more info, something revealing about the name Cornelius related to the Academy, we would have got it, provided if we look in the Administrative Database. So the problem now, I think, is that, with Sally's advice in mind, looking in the Administrative Database, we won't find it. Looking in neither the Academy Administration Database nor the Library will provide results. My head started to hurt, maybe it's time to get fresh one. Maybe Adam will have some insight.

I headed to the cafeteria and hope to find Adam eating his pre-dinner meal. I entered the large white-tiled cafeteria. The cafeteria was huge, ambient lighting, nice kitchen/bar, and plenty of tables with chairs that seemed to overpopulate the number of people eating at any given time. I found him, eating at the center of the room. At the center of the group of tables there were six tables surrounding the absolute center of the room, which look like any other passage, but it's hard to miss that when you look at the chaos of the arrangement of the tables of the cafeteria. "Hey Adam," I called.

Adam was with his laptop hacking away and eating his nuggets from the small bowl. "Hey," Adam muffled. "Trying to hack in, but I can't find anything, well I can't get at the same server, there's something that's rerouting me."

Then I thought, well Sally must know something about this, I believe what Adam was experiencing is what Sally meant, we're looking at the obvious place, the right place where the information has to be, the library and the Administrative Database, places where information about a person would supposed to be. The information we are looking for is at the wrong place. "Hey," I paused, "I had a talk with Sally."

"Lovely," Adam replied dryly.

"Too busy?" I asked.

"No, I'm still listening, I'm focused now," Adam explained. "I want to know what's all this about, and luckily you gave me an opportunity."

"Look, that talk with Sally," I reported. "She told me, well us in a way, that if we keep looking here, at those places, we will keep coming up empty handed."

"You trust her on that?" Adam asked. "You got knocked out with that race with her, from what you told me about her and you, she's seems cynical, she might be throwing us off."

"Like that system you're playing with?" I asked.

He stopped and looked at me. "What do you mean?" Adam asked.

"The information we want, is not in where we think information would be," I explained and smiled.

"Where it is?" Adam asked. "Since I'm doing the hacking, I need a guide, some direction."

"The information is at the wrong place," I said. "That's all I got from what Sally said, well deciphered what she said."

"Okay, one question," Adam sighed. "What would be the wrong place to find info about Cornelius who is related to the Academy founding and this building. If his info, well the one we want is not in the Academy's website, then where would it be?"

"The website is from the server at the Admin building," I smiled. "The library database is not at the library itself."

"So it's here at the Academy," Adam sighed. "But the admin is part of the Academy."

"True," I paused, I just came to an epiphany. "But that's what we know and see of the Academy."

"Okay go on," Adam said intrigued.

"But that means, the direction we want to head to, knowing what the Academy is, is the direction, is the clue," I paused. "We have to look in the Academy that also means it's far more than we thought it was."

"Okay granted if that's the right direction for me to look," Adam said. "How do I hack to it?"

"I have a feeling you can't from here," I explained. "We have to get closer."

"To what?" Adam asked. "The center of this apparent conspiracy."

I stared at center of the six tables. “No, more like void of our understanding,” I said.

Chapter 6- Breaking the Rules
9/26-28/03

10:05:26 PM
-9/26/06-

Some information can be misleading. Sally might be misleading us to something horrible. If she is, then that means I won't be able to compete against her, and she made it clear that with me, there is no point in competing. Things are just scattered and I'm here trying to put the giant jig-saw puzzle together. I needed some help to find out who the hell are those two dealers. After they left I continued up to my room on the fourth floor. As soon as I got into my room, I headed to the phone; started to call a friend of mine that could help me solve this once in for all, Scotty Turgeon. "Who is it?" he called.

"It's Bryan," I replied.

He groaned. "God! I all ready paid your fifty dollars!" he growled.

"This is different," I yawned, "I need you to get some dirt on someone."

"Who?" he asked.

"Sally," I replied.

"That one scary girl?" Scotty asked.

"Yeah, I want to know what her deal with me is," I explained. "Can you do that?"

"What do you mean?" Scotty asked.

"I want to know why she wants to keep competing with me," I explained.

"Why you want to know that?" he asked.

"It's been bugging me for a while," I replied.

"What am I getting out of this?" Scotty asked.

"The fifty bucks you gave me," I smiled.

"Alright, I'll see what I can do," Scotty sighed. "Bye."

I have a feeling that Scotty may be getting himself into trouble, so I hope the fifty dollars would cover such trouble, but just in case I should trail behind.

-9/27/03- Morning 5:35:05

This morning was calm and smooth compared to yesterdays. Things at the Academy were calm. Regular weekend classes, no accidents, no media jerks, no nothing, just peace; Words I'll regret writing, thinking and saying immediately. During breakfast I met up with Sierra and Devon munching down on some waffles. "Hey, what's up," I greeted with a smile.

"Nothing much," Sierra replied.

"Just getting ready for a day of nothing!" Devon cheered.

"Yeah," I sighed. "I know it's our day off, it will be our several class free Saturdays for the next five weeks," I reported.

"That's great!" Devon said before munching down on the waffles.

"So, I heard you were doing some snooping," Sierra pointed. "How is that going?"

"Adam told you?" I asked.

"If you called it that, then yes, Adam told me," Sierra smiled.

"What did you do?" I asked.

"Gave him a noogie," Sierra chuckled.

"Ah, okay," I paused. "Yeah, we are doing some investigating about the Academy and a person named 'Cornelius'."

"Adam got you paranoid?" Devon asked.

"No, but he has a point about the inconsistencies about this place," I stated.

"Something like that might get you into trouble," Sierra said. "That is of course considering the fact that you are working with him alone."

"I got Scotty working on it also," I added.

"Scotty?" Sierra asked. "He's just a gearhead, just knows, well mechanical things and stuff like that, nothing near the realm of intel, puzzles."

"Puzzles are what he is good at," I stated. "Following people is easy, yes he's mechanically inclined, hence he's puzzle solver, and machines are nothing but puzzles."

"So you think this is some sort of machine like ordeal?" Devon asked. "Seems a bit of a stretch for comparison."

"No, not like a machine, just we're seeing one machine, part of many," I explained. "It's a system were looking at. I have a feeling it's far larger than we thought, and the Academy is the center of it, or at least close to it."

"You're just jumping into this blind are you?" Devon asked.

"That's the thing, I don't know, all we can do, if I want to know what's up, is to take a leap of faith," I explained.

"You sound determined," Devon stated. "Though that can be just paranoia, but you know what the hell if Adam is in, I'm glad to help."

Devon looked at Sierra. "What about you?" Devon asked.

"Might as well, to keep Adam in line," Sierra sighed.

"Then it's settled, you have your crew behind you one hundred percent," Devon stated, "What's the first thing to do?"

"Wait for what Adam digs up from his search," I stated.

"Really?" Sierra asked. "That's all right now?"

"Yeah," I said. "We can't really do anything right now."

"We can think," Sierra stated.

"Okay," I paused. "Think about what?"

"Look, This somewhat involves the Academy, obviously, and it involves then programs the Academy has, Cornelius must be tied to one of the programs here. And what Sally said to you about looking in the wrong place for what you need," Sierra paused. "What if it means we are looking at it the wrong way?"

"Okay," I nodded. "Sure, what is the right way?"

"The one that leads us forward, progress," Sierra smiled.

"She has a point, and it might work," Devon paused. "Except, what is the right way?"

"What program Cornelius is connected to," Sierra stated. "Yes he might have been an administrator here, but he contributes to a program a lot."

"We might find what we want there," I nodded. "Okay, what program?"

"Uh, guys," Adam interrupted. "I might have that answer."

I turned around and Adam was standing there with his laptop in his hand and an exhausted face and a small noticeable frown. "What happened?" I asked. "Was it that much hacking?" I asked.

"Oh, no," Adam perked up. "It's just I'm still shaken from Sierra's small interrogation earlier."

"That bad?" I asked.

"You have no idea," Adam sighed.

I turned to Sierra and she just gave me a cutesy innocent smile. "I have my ways," she chuckled.

"Remind me to never withhold anything from you," I sighed.

"Withholding information from her is not the problem," Adam explained. "She'll do it for the fun of it."

"You're insane," I said dryly to Sierra.

"You're just paranoid," she quipped.

"I," I paused. "That's not the point, anyways, what do you have Adam."

"Well, I found more information about Cornelius in the Academy sea of data banks," Adam sighed.

"Well that's good, where at?" I asked.

"Science and Technology," Adam replied. "It was right under our noses."

"In our program, well where exactly?" Sierra asked. "In the classes or the training?"

"See that's the problem I'm trying to convey to you guys," Adam stopped. "Though it was my fault in not expressing it well enough for you to understand or know that there was a problem."

"Well you just did now," Devon sighed. "Spill it, smalls."

"Don't call me that," Adam sighed as he sat down. "The trail ended when I was automatically locked out of some servers, and was redirected to some areas of the data network."

"Okay?" I asked.

"The security system was fast and well coded to do that, but what I could uncover was that what is going on that causes the weird sense of oddness in our program was really under our noses," Adam explained. "There's another program, connecting every class and training session in our program, a secret network, only that none of the teachers and administrators other than Cornelius have direct access to this secret network."

"What's in the network?" Sierra asked.

"One program," Adam replied. "I couldn't get the full name of the program but I got some of the side project, well one big project collaboration, Hive."

"Hive?" I asked. "What you found out about that?"

"It's a big project, it's in here, in this Academy, and in its system," Adam continued. "Logs about the project, I have them here in my hard drive, and all of them were documents, authorization papers all signed by Cornelius."

"We have his last name too?" Devon asked eagerly.

"No, he just signed Cornelius," Adam answered. "And oh, I found some logs about a Waynesboro Incident."

"That's where you and Sierra were the other day," Devon stated. "What happened?"

"I don't know," I replied. "The incident was far from the station, it was at some Academy Administration Facility."

"It was a computing facility, data storage for the Science and Technology Program in The Academy," Adam corrected.

"Why was it at Waynesboro?" Devon asked.

"Something is still there," Sierra stated. "The next clue to this confusing mystery."

"But we have to break the rules," Adam stated.

I stopped and thought about that, Adam wasn't wrong about the rules and regulation. But if we are going to find out what's going on here, we have to ignore some rules. "Listen," Adam sighed. "If what the logs say were accurate, I'm sure we are going too far down the rabbit hole and won't survive what will be there waiting for us. I mean, the bombing, b-o-m-b-i-n-g, at the Waynesboro place, someone has deadly force and I'm not willing to be caught in the line of fire."

"Adam has a point," Devon sighed.

It was strange to listen to Adam as a voice of reason, and wondered what really happened. At first we were all riled up from Adam's suspicion and finally galvanized ourselves to find out the truth. Now the initiator seemed to be shocked, paralyzed. "Adam what you found exactly?" I asked.

"Project files, but they seemed to be heavily encrypted, some sort of hex code," Adam explained.

"Hex?" Sierra asked, "Like a curse?"

"No," I said. "I think he meant six, a hexagonal code, six-figured based code."

"Where in The Academy would they need a code like that?" Devon asked.

"Somewhere in the Tech program," I explained. "A place where we don't have easy access to, even if we are allowed near..."

"The Yards," Sierra pointed out. "There some sheds and workshops we are not allowed near or in, but I can't be that simple, there has to be a secret or hidden way to enter them without us noticing."

"We have to break the rules to find out," Devon sighed, "which is good because I'm kinda getting tired of the regulations at the Yard."

"Where would something like that be?" I asked.

Sierra turned to Adam. "He knows," Sierra said dryly.

"Adam?" I asked. "Care enough to fill us in more?"

"You know," Adam sighed. "I'm getting tired, and I'm very uncomfortable with this."

"It's your fault I'm this intrigued and this far in this rabbit hole," I stated.

"Well I have a feeling that we were already deep in the rabbit hole," Adam paused. "We just are now acknowledging it. Anyways there is a clue I got out of attempting to crack the encrypted code, it was just a number, '1950', and a city 'Norfolk'."

"The portal to the records is at Norfolk?" Devon asked.

"Well I guess," Adam shrugged. "Its portal that might eventually lead to the files we are after."

"So this Hive Project is at Norfolk?" Sierra asked.

"I think so," Adam sighed.

They turned to me, I was deep into thought, I was staring at the red velvet floor, thinking deeply. 1950. Norfolk. Seemed to be a long stretch, very vague clues Adam pulled out from the code. I was think that maybe it was a building built in 1950 in Norfolk, but that would imply that it was on some military installation. Since Norfolk was at the naval bases in Virginia, the 1950 maybe referred to the year a building was built as a measure for the Cold War. "Also," Adam interrupted. "It requires a password to unencrypted, seven characters."

"Any hints?" I asked.

"Steel," Adam sighed. "It's like this code is like a poem, very strange, well elegant, the computer geek who did this has a lot of time on their hands."

"Like you on Saturdays?" Sierra asked.

"I thought he was like that all the time," Devon joked.

"Steel," I softly repeated.

"You got anything?" Adam asked.

"Nope," Sierra sighed.

"Not a clue," Devon scratched his head.

"Type western," I said.

"Why?" Adam asked. "Are you sure?"

"Positive, besides, like you said we're in the rabbit hole, dark and only two ways to go forward and back, and it just takes a blind leap forward to make progress."

"You are starting to scare me," Adam sighed.

"He's just adventurous," Sierra stated. "Type the word."

Adam slowly typed the word and hit entered and waited for the screen to load up. "He might also be blindsided by this conspiracy feeling," Sierra added.

For a full minute the computer screen did not load up. Adam sighed and shook his head. "We tried," he paused. "Well it was good run let's all go back to our normal lives!"

The computer screen lit up, a hexagon was in the middle of the screen, multiple windows popped up with lists of names and words filling it, scrolling down. The loading ended quickly and the hexagon in the middle bud a window with a blank search box. "What is this?" Adam asked.

"The lantern to our rabbit hole," Sierra smiled.

"Type Cornelius," I ordered. "We don't know if it's going to lock us out soon."

"It won't," Adam reported. "We are in, we are permanently in, there's no turning back."

Adam typed in Cornelius and a bunch of files filled the screen. These files were transfer files for students of the Academy signed by Cornelius, all of them involved with secret projects like Hive and HPR. "Adam you have work today," I said.

"I know," Adam sighed. "I have it done by tomorrow."

"Wait, what's that popping up?" Devon pointed

There was a window popping up at the corner of the screen, it was message with no signature. It read: No personnel at sheds tomorrow, security systems will be down, window of opportunity available to reach files. "What shed?" I asked.

Another window popped below: 1950, Norfolk and Western that is all I can give. The windows disappeared. But the files remained. "That was strange," Devon scoffed. "This clue this is starting to be boring and annoying."

"1950," I whispered.

"Looks like we're heading to Norfolk," Sierra smiled. "I'll get ready."

"I don't think it's in Norfolk," I stated. "It's here."

"Okay where?" Sierra asked sassily.

"1950, Norfolk and Western," I stated. "It's in a locomotive shed, the *Black Bullet*."

"How did you?" Devon asked.

"The *Black Bullet* was build in 1950, well this one and it was built and commissioned by the Norfolk and Western Railroad."

"So the entrance in the shed, where?" Devon asked.

"The ashpan, it's deep enough," I smiled.

"So it's settled tomorrow afternoon then" Sierra smiled.

Everyone agreed tomorrow afternoon was the best time, since it was the only time of the day that the shed is empty and the systems were down to do routine checks. We went our separate ways I went back to my room to relax during the rest of the day. But as I walked down the residential hallway I felt a chill on my spine, I turned around thinking someone was following me but I was just paranoid I looked at the ceiling looking for cameras but I didn't find any, well the visible obvious black ones, maybe there some hidden ones like in the exit sign or in the decorative molding. As I reached my dorm, I found an envelope with Sally's handwriting on it. I pulled it off and felt that there was a card inside, a red card with a golden hexagon printed on it. It shined in the light and I turned it and twirled it. When I got inside I saw I had a message for me. I quickly pressed the play button and it was Scotty. "Hey Bryan, you know the task you put me to do? Well I lost track of her, Sally disappeared, I know you might think I lost her or I didn't do this right, but really he room has been cleared out and her name disappeared from the sign in sheets at the classes at the Academy," Scotty paused. "All I got was a letter from her saying 'He know what to do with it.' Dude, I think you are on your own. Whatever it is you have to do, or what she expects you to do, you might have to break some rules along the way."

So be it then.

Chapter 7: The Hunt Begins
9/29/03
01:25:30 AM

We met up with Adam in his room analyzing the information we hacked. “So Adam got anything yet?” I asked.

“No not really,” Adam yawned. “Oh, wait, here's something.”

“What it is?” I asked.

“Transfer files,” Adam replied. “Of your friend.”

I looked at the monitor and saw it was transfer files of Sally; she was heading off to the El Paso Academy. “She transferred?” I asked.

“Yup,” Adam smiled. “Yesterday, too and it was quick.”

“I suspect they were getting rid of people from here,” I sighed.

“Yup and making placing them somewhere else in the system,” Adam paused. “All the files I looked over like this, there were people like us and Sally.”

“Okay where are you going with this?” I asked.

“Sally might knew something they kept her away from it,” Adam explained. “I mean.”

“So they kidnapped her?” I asked. “To keep her quiet?”

“Yes,” Adam nodded, “Exactly that.”

“Well how about this,” I paused. “She knew what’s here, but she was sent to another campus where they actually do the things that they are hiding here.”

“I’m sorry I got lost after ‘Well’,” Adam apologized.

“What if,” I sighed, “What is here, or the programs here are just the central distribution system of what’s going on, information about the entire system is here.”

“Conspiracy much?” Adam asked.

I slammed the pass card on to his desk. “Sally gave it to me,” I sighed. “She left a note in my room and Scotty lost track of her, but sent me a log of her whereabouts before she got transferred.”

“And you assume we are the guinea pigs,” Adam paused. “The guinea pigs of this academy?”

“The point is that what’s Sally is trying to find out,” I pointed out. “Where ever she was there might be a clue she left for us to find and take it on.”

“But I thought she hated you,” Adam scratched his head.

“She needed me to create a false sense to whatever system is out there around us, that we were just competing, like academic jocks,” I explained.

“Then why are we not falling victim to what Sally fell to in this ‘system’,” Adam asked.

“Because we are the exception,” I gasped.

“What?” Adam asked.

“That’s why we feel awkward here, because we are not in sync with the system the Academy has in place!” I explained. “We are like ghosts in the system, a glitch as you might understand it. We can do things she can’t, and the illusion that Sally thinks that I can beat her because I have the upper hand was just that!”

“Why we are the exception?” Adam asked.

“Because of the system,” I smiled, “and now exactly what we are looking for.”

“How the system is set up and what is going down,” Adam nodded. “Okay, it’s set then.”

Sierra walked in, and we both noticed she was worried and carried the face of *I have bad news*. “Guys we might have a problem,” she sighed. “Devon tested out some security systems.”

“Where is he?” I asked.

“Disciplinary Office,” Sierra sighed.

“We, well, he got caught taking the tram unauthorized,” Sierra paused. “I jumped from the tram and high tailed it back here without anyone chasing me."

"How are we going to get to the entrance?" I asked.

"There must be some way to get there," Sierra paused and looked at me. "You have a higher ranking than us. You're a crew chief you can go down there without noticing."

"True," I nodded. "But I can't take anyone else without authorization."

"Yup, it'll take too long for permission," Adam pointed. "Even if we break regulations and go ahead use his cover, we'll be toast like Devon. He'll go alone."

"Why him?" Sierra asked.

"Because I know what we are looking for," I explained, "Something that explains the system, something what explains everything about the program."

"We'll be here then," Sierra added. "Adam can give you an earpiece and we can sort the info you dig up."

I turned to Adam. "You have that type of equipment?" I asked.

"He used to be a spy boy back in Vegas," Sierra smiled. "Dreaming to work for the Air Force, or casino, whatever pays him more?"

"Okay," I said. "That's good to hear."

Adam went to his closet and pullout a black suitcase. He opened it and it was filled with spy gadgets you can buy from a 2-bit electronics store. "Here's an earpiece," Adam paused. "And a PDA with an internet link, for the information you will dig up."

"Okay," I nodded. "Thanks, what you do Sierra?"

"We'll stay here and help him out, but first I'm going to try to get Devon out," Sierra announced. "Good luck."

Sierra left quickly and walked briskly down the stairs. I walked out of Adam's room and started my way to where Sally was last first traced by Scotty. I looked at the notepad he had when he was following her. The last entry was of him following Sally into the library. He spotted her at the science section, at Aisle 23, shelf case 5. "Adam, can you hear me?" I asked.

"Loud and clear," Adam replied.

"I'm heading over to the Library first," I announced.

"What for?" he asked.

"Got a lead from Scotty's notes of Sally's whereabouts, she was last seen at the Library in the Science and Technology Section," I explained. "Maybe she left something in the books."

"Which is it?" Adam asked. "You'll spend too much time there finding that damn clue, but hey make it quick you're the one doing this solo mission. I'll be on standby."

"Roger," I agreed.

Adam was right, strange to say that, I can't spend too much time there looking for this phantom clue, part of me thinks that there isn't a clue there, and Sally was there to throw Scotty off because she knew he was following her. Then again that same tactic maybe her only way of communicating what she needed to tell me without accelerating her sudden transfer. All of this seems beyond suspicious, but I hope the passage, room or whatever I'm going to after the library will have the answers I'm looking for, what all of us are looking for. I made way through the hallow hallways of the Manor and found the Library partially empty, a few student's reading and on the computer hubs around the dark granite columns. I walked by the towering bookcases of the library. They were lined with stainless steel corners and chrome signs with faux copper lettering. I went to Aisle 23 and found bookcase 5, and began looking at the lower shelves. All the books among the lower shelves had similar colors, some pale blue, dark dusty blue, green, and black. They all are either manuals, transcripts, journals published about whatever scientific subject this shelf is about. I picked a random book and it read: Principles of Atomic Physics, First Edition. "Great Sally," I sighed. "More riddles?"

I put my hand in my pocket and began to walk out of the aisle when I felt the card key. I pulled it out and saw there was a hidden holographic number sequence with six digits: 640219. I began to walk back and look for the corresponding numbers inside books. Then I found an oddly colored book, it was bright green, I looked inside, the last digits of the ISBN were a matched, it was book about J. Robert Oppenheimer, there was note card on the first page and it read "Tesla was out of place, but was meant to be there."

It was written in Sally's handwriting, and I began to look for a book, maybe it was out of place, hidden from a normal glance, but if you were looking for it you'll find it. Then I stood still, in the middle of the bookcase's length, at the shelf that was eye level with me was thick book, orange pushed in the spine of the book was further back than the others. The spine of the orange book read Tesla with silver lettering. I pulled out the book I turned to the first page, it was empty. The next one only had a single line of text, it read "The present is theirs; the future, for which I really worked for, is mine." I closed the book, and noticed the thickness of the book and the weight of it, it was light for the number of pages it had. I opened the book quickly, from the middle, and I discovered it was hollowed. There was a stainless steel plate in the shape of a hexagon. I picked up the plate and noticed in the lighting, the finished lines of the hexagonal stainless steel plate, made a hexagon grid. I rubbed my fingers on the surface of the plate gently and felt the faint, soft lines of the hidden grid. I quickly put the plate in my backpack and the book too, and headed my way out. "Hey Adam," I called.

"Hey, you found what Sally left?" he asked.

"Yea," I paused, "An orange book and a stainless steel plate in a shape of a hexagon about a half of an inch thick hidden in the book. Seemed hollow the plate, but I can't open it."

"We'll figure something out," Adam replied. "In the meantime, I suggest heading to the shed quickly our window of opportunity is closing."

"Roger that," I nodded. "I'm heading to the tram station now."

I walked out the side entrance down the bricked walkway through the Library garden on the side of the manor overlooking the yards. I entered the tram station and swiped my card and the light turned green, the gates unlocked and I pushed my through the gate tumbler. I sat in the tram, as more of the people from the Academy were getting on to go to their classes down in the yard. "Are you going to class?" one of them asked.

"Yeah," I nodded. "Basic Mechanics, love that class, I'm thinking staying afterwards to work on my project."

"Oh cool what is your project?" the guy asked enthusiastically.

I froze and panicked. My mouth was open like a fish about to eat bait. "Well, um I," I stuttered.

I had to come up with something or say something quick, before they became suspicious. "Well," I paused. "Let me find the words to explain it."

I bought myself a few seconds with that, and the tram was about to stop at the yards. "All I can say," I paused again and looked at the front of the tram, as the station was just feet away. "The best I can describe it, my project of mine is...that it's...an engine."

"What type?" he asked quickly.

The tram came to a halt as it was at the yard station already. As I got up I smiled at him. "I can't tell you," I said. "It's kinda under wraps, still a work in progress."

"Of course, you haven't made it," he nodded. "You have the idea; you are now just going to manifest it with your two hands. That is why you're here."

I stood there and I felt a rush throughout my body, the same feeling when Adam was talking about the strangeness of this place came over me. I paused a little while, I was occupied with the strange feeling, I hesitated to answer. Eventually I did, faster than my last response though. "Yes," I smiled. "That's why."

I quickly got off the tram and briskly headed my way to the shed. The other guy headed off in a different direction; once I was out of sight from the people who got off the tram I slowed down my walk and casually walked into the shed where the *Black Bullet* was parked at. The large beastly engine was glimmering in its streamlined black skin. "Okay Adam," I called. "I'm in the shed, no one is here."

"That's good news," Adam cheered. "You found the entrance?"

"Not yet," I replied. "But I'm thinking like Sally now and looking for a hidden spot."

"Okay?" Adam paused. "Whatever works, man."

I looked around, nothing really movable, like a hidden switch, nothing in the ash pits beneath the engine. I looked towards the back, at the corner near where the crew of the locomotive hangs out. The bench and small stool table were untouched from the crew that was here. At the very corner I saw a vending machine with no cash slot, nor a coin slot. I took a quick look at it and found it only accepted a card, on the lip of the card slot was a golden hexagon like the one on the card Sally gave me. I pulled out the card from my pocked and slid it into the card slot, it clicked. The entire vending machine clicked, the card pushed back, and I placed in my pocket. The front end of the vending machine opened; there was a cage that was rising up. The cage stopped, I opened the cage and walked in the creaks were silent much like the mice that run through the sheds in the darkness of the nightshift. I closed the cage, I pulled a lever next to me and the cage slowly began to descend, the vending machine began to close. When I was at eye level to the floor the front end of the vending machine shut. The small light bulb in the cage was the only source of illumination. I could barely see the dirty walls of the small shaft with the equally spaced air vents that I passed by on my way down. "Adam," I called. "I think I found the passage."

"Gre-I-ah-ood," Adam said.

"Adam you're breaking up," I replied.

"I-ant-ear-," Adam replied.

I could only hear static and the scratchiness of his voice due to the electrical interference. Then suddenly I could only hear static, I switched off the ear piece. "Well," I sighed. "I'm on my own."

I pulled out the PDA and found that I wasn't receiving an internet signal down here. I was on my own from here on. The elevator stopped, but I could not see what's in front of me. Then I heard loud clicks lights turned on, I turned around, the gate behind me opened and there was a long corridor, lined with red bricks. The corridor was tube shaped, lined with red bricks at the connection supports. The walls between the supports were a dull green and the tiles on the floor were a dirty smooth gray. I walked down and saw the lights; they were dirty brass arc lamps that poorly lit the corridor. As I walked by several illuminated spots, I heard a very loud thump; the elevator behind me was closed off by a concrete barrier. I felt the thump all over my body, the loud thump still rang in my ears when I heard faint buzzing, and it grew gradually and stopped as another set of lights turned on. The second set of lights was brighter, but they were not exactly cylindrical like the arc lamps. These were thicker at the middle, like an old fashioned fluorescent light bulb. I could see the wires that powered the lights snaked along the wall and ceiling portion held by iron clamps. I saw the pipe work too snaked down the corridor, but it was in an orderly manner, they were all connected by a special elbow making zigzag patterns, they were not the ninety degree elbows, they were a smaller degree, some sixty and thirty to my guessing. The pipes were grimy and a dull brown, all held up or to the wall by the same iron clamps for the wires but they were bigger.

I kept continuing down the corridor and heard a faint humming from deeper in the corridor. As I followed the sound I came to an intersection, three directions, forward, left or right; at the end of each direction, in what seems to be at an equal distance from me where doors. They all had a heavy duty locking mechanism built on to the door. The doors were covered with dark evergreen gears, rods, cams and bolts. They were clean compared to the corridors condition. I heard the humming and hissing coming from the door the left, so naturally I headed to the door on the left. As I got closer to the door there was a valve in the middle of all the mechanisms around it. There was a dirty white plate behind the handle of the valve with a red arrow pointing in the clockwise direction. I looked back and around, I noticed the lining of the tubular corridor changed. About eight feet from the door the corridor walls were a dull rusty brown with deep grooves in a spiral direction. The walls were protected by a smaller cage in a tubular fashion. I pulled the handle of the valve to the right. The walls began to turn, rotate around me the floor began to move forward. The door's gears rotated clicked and grinded as the entire section moved. Two feet forward the doors began to slid open and began to move along sides of the concrete platform. They moved past me and closed at the end of the platform as it moved forward the full eight feet. The loud clank and thump rattled my body. I looked forward and there was larger corridor, a tunnel really. I took a step forward and heard a loud click and saw the handle of the valve was back at its original position. The loud hissing was right here. I looked to the side and saw a large machine with pipes and valves, it was running, air was being pumped by that machine. "Where is it pumping it to?" I thought to myself. The platform shook and jolted; the platform slowly began to move forward, the gears of the doors were running but they were detached from the platform. I heard a dull humming from below. The tunnel was illuminated and I saw in the middle of the track was a tube of some sort; I saw blasts of air coming from the tube in the middle of the track. "It's a pneumatic train," I gasped. "Wow, underground too, this is strange."

The platform charged forward, flying by the tunnels supports and wall mounted wires, pipes and lanterns. It gradually came to a stop to a platform with a low ceiling and bright white lights. I climbed to the platform and saw a circular door, but in a shape of a gear with six braces radiating from the center circular panel. The center panel didn't have any screens, buttons or slots it was slab of polished concrete. "I wonder," I whispered.

I pushed it. That's all I did, I pushed it. The door clicked and pushed towards me and stopped and rotated to the right, there was a room, it was a vault. I walked by the strange vault door and into the vault. There I saw boxes and boxes placed along metal shelves. I saw a row of computers, well just really flat monitors on tables. Then I saw a large panel of glass mounted on the dirty dark concrete wall of the vault. All the shelves were pointed at it, as it was radiating from it. The glass panel was just that, a glass panel, part of a large brass thin (for its size) box. In front was a small panel control stand. In the middle was button. Again I pressed it. Two halves of a keyboard came from the sides of the panel stand and came together on top of the panel. The screen flicked, there was bunch of windows popping up but one came up in the center. A small black screen, white text appeared, it read “Box 458i, contents inside.”

I looked back and spotted the only box that was off centered and not straight. It was labeled with an orange sticker reading “Box 458i”. I popped off the lid, inside were black folders with white tabs. I saw Sally’s name on the tabs, I grabbed it and read through all the files. There were paperwork and applications in the file, but all of them were blank, they just had Sally’s name and date of birth on all of the applications. Then I came across a page of paperwork, all of the fields were blacked out but at the field at the bottom, the box that read Comments, only one word: “Listen.”

“Listen?” I asked myself.

“Yes you should,” a voice agreed.

I turned around and saw the screen cleared out, just a black screen with white text in the middle, that read. “Yes you should.”

“Who are you?” I asked.

The screen showed another line of white text: “Ha-ha”. Then another one along with the voice, “Ha-ha,” The voice said, “First time I was asked that.”

Another line of text popped up, but it was some sort of computer command line. “The voice quietly said. “Syncing Peripherals Alpha Ten.”

I stepped closer to the panel and stared at the screen. Then I heard gears rotating and clicking behind me. It was a crude robotic arm, made from steel frames, iron gears, cams, rods, powered by miniature Tesla turbines with hoses running the length of the arm to the ceiling. At the end was a small camera, it had a green glow and it was staring at me looking up and down. The arm rotated around me and stopped in front of me, in between the panel control and the screen. "Ah, well I'm okay now, it's been a while since I had to do this," the voice said.

"Who are you?" I asked.

"Cornelius," he spoke. "The one you were looking for."

"You're Cornelius?" I asked. "Where are you?"

"Well you can say I'm a bit out of reach physically from here," Cornelius responded. "I'm tied up in the Main administration building."

"Okay," I nodded. "So you can see me, but I can't see you."

"I'm sorry it can't work both ways, but it's the best I can do with all that's happening," Cornelius sighed.

"What's happening?" I asked.

"The currents under your feet," Cornelius replied. "But now that you descended into them, it'll be logical for me to tell."

"How bad is it?" I asked.

"Beyond what you can imagine," Cornelius answered.

"I came here to look for Sally's whereabouts and what the Academy is all about," I protested. "I'm not here to get involved."

"Yet you did when you began to question the state of the Academy, asking why things are the way they are," Cornelius responded. "Though there is no punishment from my direction, it's not in my nature to do so. In fact you came to the right place. But about your friend and your question about the Academy, what's happening involves that deeply."

"How so," I asked, "Who actually took Sally?"

"I did, for her safety," Cornelius responded.

The robotic arm went to the left a little bit and the screen flickered on with windows popping up and showing a picture of a person, with description and a website of a company. “I transferred Sally out of this Academy to the one in El Paso,” Cornelius explained. “It involved the HPR, which sadly I don’t know much. All I know is that Sally uncovered some filed about the HPR and a link to a military contracted company. That I know. What I showed you here, is Abrecan Gunther, CEO of Falcon Industries. I’m trying to figure out their connections to the Academy but I can’t, since I’m only limited to the oversight of students of the Academy.”

“So you’re not in charge of the Academy?” I asked.

“No,” Cornelius sighed. “I was then I was placed in the overseeing you student’s welfare, hence why I was able to get your friend to safety.”

“Okay,” I nodded.

“Anyways, this mans, this company of his,” Cornelius paused. “Has connections to the HPR but I do not know what, but that’s not where the problems lies. His contracts with the military make are possible form his weapons engineering. Where we come in is there. I know that some students are involved with research on their own, creating projects and tinker with them advancing their education, hence why the Academy was founded. Not too long ago, a student was working on a project, a computer project called Queen Bee, the next step in computing, very smart kid. Though now I can’t find the kid’s name in my databases, and the paper trail is gone. Though traces of his project remains, The Hive.”

“That’s great and all,” I interrupted. “But I’m going to go after Sally.”

“They will trace you to find her,” Cornelius warned. “They will get there faster than you and it’ll be too late and the Academy will cease to exist.”

"Why is that?" I asked. "Why would the Academy go away?"

"Because of the Hive they are looking for," he explained. "The student who designed the project, when he graduated he worked for Falcon Industries, he created an alternate version of the Queen Bee, The Hive the student called it. But he gave them a watered-down faulty version of the machine to Falcon Industries weapons engineering, though it still worked, but it limited the great possibilities it gave to the future prototypes of the project. Before the student graduated he built the actual machine hidden around here in the mountains around the Academy. I guess that Gunther is looking for it right now, it's been years he's been looking for it, and I think he may found a lead."

"So what will happen to the Academy when he does find it?" I asked.

"It'll be gone," Cornelius sighed in sadness. "The program will cease to exist, you and I will not exist I'm afraid."

"Why?" I asked.

"I don't know exactly," Cornelius replied. "He's planning a hostile takeover of the HPR and the Hive, and HPR has a large hand in the Academy, we just will go away and become part of whatever they are planning to do."

"That is?" I asked.

"Something bad," Cornelius replied. "That's why I need you. You see if you want to know more about the Academy, it has to stand and with the Falcon Industries take over that'll ruin the chance for you to find the truth."

"That's true," I nodded. "But how will I stop their plans?"

"Like I said, I suspected that Gunther may have found the location of the Hive," Cornelius continued. "He's probably having his moving party making the facility all nice and clean, gutting the exterior of The Hive. You can disrupt the process, make it a big deal and, well, make them hit the Academy in a way where we can get sympathy; at least it'll buy us sometime for the Administration to square things off with Mr. Gunther."

"That's all?" I asked. "Still I'm looking for answers about the Academy."

"I can reassure you that finding The Hive and remains of the Queen Bee project will help you understand the Academy better and your place, what you're feeling and what you will find, well hunt down I'm saying that due to your persistent nature for these things, will come together and make sense," Cornelius replied. "But now you need to stop this!"

"Sally was in danger because of this," I stated. "How do you know I won't be harmed like her if she wasn't transferred?"

"You're the exception," he said. "They don't know you; they don't know you're on the hunt. You're the exception, you can do this."

"You sound so confident about that I can do this without harm to me," I stated. "But okay, where do I begin, um, hunting?"

"The north yards, near the old mine," Cornelius stated. "Here's a map of possible locations of entrances to the Hive's vault. Also, I know you can do this, since I'm charge of overseeing the student's talents, skills, abilities and progress in the Academy. I have all the facts that you are capable of completing this task and finding out what the Academy is about. Plus your new crewmates are a special bunch, without them you won't be here. Before you go, you might need these."

The panel control popped up and opened itself, revealing another hexagon like the one I got. "You might need this other one," Cornelius said. "I knew Sally was going to give you the one she found in the mountains the other day. This will help you, and, I'm uploading all the information about this conversation and the situation at hand to your PDA, once you get back in range send that to Adam, I'm also giving you all the encrypted info I got to you, in hope that you will crack it. Now go and goodbye."

"Wait," I called. "Will we still be in contact? Or do I have to come here?"

"You'll know how when you need me," Cornelius chuckled.

The screen flickered off the robotic hand moved up and I proceed to move to the tunnel, once I was out I felt the PDA vibrate. I took it out and there was a message on the screen. "Do you want be a Rocketeer for a moment, take the platform down, there is a special shaft leading back to the academy, hitch a ride on the backpack up." I stepped on the platform as I was reading this. "What?" I asked myself.

The platform dropped, I grabbed onto the railings as the platform descended deeper into the ground. The platform stopped and there was a small hallway leading to a large abandoned silo, or an air shaft. I saw a backpack with a rocket to it, it was a rocket backpack attached to a railing system. "Oh, I see now," I gasped.

I quickly strapped myself to the backpack. I placed the helmet on. "Okay what now?" I asked.

I stood there for a few seconds when the Rockets ignited. I was launched into the air, guided by the rail I flew up and up towards the end of the shaft. The rocket stopped I came to a stop, the rail twisted around and I found myself a step away from the top platform. "That should be an amusement park ride," I laughed to myself.

I looked at the door and opened it just to find myself in another hallway with a familiar door at the end. I went forward and opened it to find myself at the

South Gardens, next to the Observation Dome of the Manor. “Whoa,” I gasped, “didn’t know that was here.”

I looked at the dome from here and it was gorgeous the glass shining under the sun. “So the hunt begins,” I said to myself. “The hunt for answers really begins.”

Chapter 8: The Discovery
9/29/03-9/30/03

-9/29/03-Late Afternoon

I gazed at the observation dome; I walked around up the stairs and into the dome. I begin to walk across the massive dome into the hallway that leads back to the main lobby of the Manor. "Bryan? Hey, can you hear me?" Adam asked.

"Yeah," I replied. "I was out."

"We know that," Adam replied. "Where were you?"

"I was out," I repeated. "You won't believe what I dug up."

"You found Cornelius?" Adam asked.

"He found me in a way," I replied.

"That's why your ear piece was out?" he asked.

"Yes," I said.

I lied, but in reality doesn't matter how the contact with Cornelius happened as long at the outcome was the same as expected if I were to tell them the truth. "He, well, spoke to me and gave me some documents, files," I explained, "I'm uploading them from the PDA."

"That's good," Adam sighed. "We thought you were gone."

"So comforting that you thought I was gone," I sighed.

"It was Sierra's idea," Adam quipped.

"And you followed?" I asked.

"She had me in a tight spot," Adam complained.

"Indian burn?" I asked.

"How did you know?" he asked.

"I heard you yelling 'Uncle, Uncle, it burns, my arm burns! Stop twisting!'" I exaggerated.

"I don't sound like a sissy," Adam complained.

"I didn't say you were a sissy, nor quoted that in a sissy voice," I stated.

"I-shut up," Adam sighed. "Okay I got the files. I'm going through them."

"I'll be in your room in a little bit," I stated.

"Okay," Adam stated.

I began my way back to Adam's room when I bumped into Evan as he was going in the opposite direction. "Watch it," he scowled. "Oh, it's *you*."

"Nice to see you Evan," I replied. "What you have been up to? It's your day off?"

"I wasn't resting, I was just doing errands, and things got tighter around her since Sally transferred," he grumbled.

It was my chance to see if anyone knows what really is going on. "Is that so?" I asked, "Why she got transferred and to where?"

"I don't know exactly why," Evan stated. "But she was transferred to one of the higher Academies, somewhere in the southwest, my guess is that she got promoted and put on the fast track."

"That's cool," I nodded. "That's great for her, she deserves it."

"Maybe so," Evan paused. "But she was acting strange lately; she was making all these detours to the Library."

"Maybe she was studying," I interrupted.

"Even you won't believe that," Evan scoffed. "No, but she's been off her game."

"Really?" I asked. "She beat me with test scores a few days ago, she was still on her game."

"Never mind," Evan scoffed. "You won't understand."

He stormed off in a hurry, fingers fiddling as he went down the stairs to the lobby. I continued my way up to Adam's room. I knocked and Devon opened it. "Sierra ditched me," Devon blurted.

"I know," I said. "She told me all about."

"And?" Devon asked.

"We might need to do teamwork trust training, the triple T's," I stated.

"When?" Devon asked.

"Our next session," I stated.

"That's in five weeks!" Devon shouted.

"I'm sorry," I apologized. "But we need to do something right now."

"I cracked all the encrypted codes on the files and they are what we are looking for," Adam reported. "Files about the Hive project, seems to be connected to-"

"The Academy," I interrupted as I sat on the edge of the bed next to Sierra.

Devon closed the door and pulled up a seat in front of us. We all gathered and sat around the computer desk in front of Adam's bed; Sierra and I on the edge of the bed, sitting Devon sitting on the side on a spare chair. "Look, this is what Cornelius told me," I explained. "Sally was transferred because she knew something and had access to a certain project that involves the Hive. The Hive is some sort of computer and tech collaboration with a company. A student that used to go here was part of the project, in fact that student created the project as part of the studies here, but now a company that hired the student betrayed that student in some way and now is looking for the original project because the version that the student game them was not the full deal."

"Okay so why things are so strange here," Adam asked.

"Us," I answered. "Sally is somehow monitored and they knew what she knew, but not us because we seemed to be the exception to this place. We seemed be the elite in reality but not recognized because of Cornelius."

"Okay what about him?" Sierra asked.

"He's in charge of the students of the Academy, not really the principal, but the like in charge of student affairs, admissions, and transfers," I explained. "But we have a problem on our hands okay, the Academy is in trouble, the company is looking for the Hive project and they may found it here on the Academy grounds, that's why things are extra strange, they might push the Academy out of existence along with us, maybe use it as a think tank."

"That's not bad," Adam nodded.

"We are going be guinea pigs and this will become a huge test chamber is we don't stop them," I sternly explained.

"Oh, that's not good," Adam retreated.

"So what are going to do?" Devon asked.

"Find the location of the Hive, the mercs for the company might of secure the area, it must be close around here, but somewhere where we can't get to easily," I stated.

"Okay and then?" Sierra asked.

"Disrupt the delivery," I said.

"If it's going be a delivery," Sierra stated. "It must be by the rail lines."

"I have a map of the possible locations," I added, "To shorten our scouting time, we will look for locations near the rail lines. Also let's see if there is a schedule of special freight trains coming by."

"That's good and all, but who are we hunting for and what?" Devon asked.

"The Hive," I stated. "It's some sort of machine and we the man we have to be on the lookout for is Abercan Gunther."

"Falcon Industries?" Adam asked. "I have a softgun from them."

"They make weapons?" Devon asked. "What the hell they want to do with us."

"Something big," I sighed. "We have to stop it."

"The delivery of the project, right," Sierra paused. "How?"

"Disrupt the traffic, waste their time, shenanigans," I smiled.

"When are we going to do this?" Devon asked.

"Tomorrow," I stated. "We have a day off."

"So it's really beginning," Adam chuckled.

-9/30/03- Mid-Morning

Thank God it was our day off! We could focus on hunting down Gunther ourselves and finding the Hive and getting it to a safe location. Sierra and Devon was in her room researching more about him. Adam and I were in the library's many small conference rooms near the reference section. "Okay, we know we can't do this with a group of four," I sighed.

"Yeah, he could rip through our skins in a second," Adam replied.

"So who else could join the crew?" I asked.

Adam squinted at the can of soda on the table. "How 'bout, Scotty," Adam replied. "Also Harley."

"Who is Harley?" I asked.

"The guy you met on the tram," Adam replied.

"Him," I nodded. "Okay, the more we can get now the better."

"True," Sierra stated.

Soon we got Scotty to join in the operation, along with Harley but with one condition, if we give him a gun. Sadly we have to do it (don't worry we only gave him an air gun disguised as a real one). Our plan was falling into place. We called both them up to meet us outside the Observation gardens. It was around twenty past eleven when the two meet us. "Here Scotty, an air gun," I smiled.

"Okay," Scotty smiled.

"Nice to meet you," Harley stated. "I might have to warn you that I'm clumsy."

"Great another one," Sierra sighed.

"Doesn't matter," I stated. "We are on a time crunch, I'm sure you will do fine."

"We all hope he does fine," Sierra grumbled.

"It doesn't matter," I stated. "We have to do this now."

"Where are going to go?" Harley asked.

"In the forest," Adam stated. "Last night I found a location near a rail line; it's near an abandoned yard to the north along the Waynesboro route, not too far from here."

"What direction we head then?" Devon asked.

"North," Adam explained. "Past the tree boundary there should be a trail near the yards in the forest."

"Alright," I smiled. "You're the navigator, let's go!"

We followed Adam into the forest and down and around the beaten trail, the sun shone through the cracks of the forested sky above us. The smell of autumn was strong in the forest now, leaves blanket the gravel trail that snakes around the thick old oak trunks of the trees that covers the sky with clouds of red, yellow and orange falling leaves. Everyone was in a single file line, Harley was picking up unique rocks and constantly catching up. "Drop them," I called out. "You don't know need them now."

"You might never know," Harley blurted. "We need some back up resources."

"At least he thinks ahead," Sierra sighed.

"Come on," I smiled. "Give the guy some slack."

We were walking for maybe two hours when we finally came across some old buildings and old machinery laying around with local landscape growing over the stationary statues of machinery.

"I guess we are at the Corvin Cave Depot," I explained. "It used to be a trolley station for the scenic hikers, before they built the trail to downtown Roanoke."

"The old yard is not too far from here," Adam pointed.

"But let's rest, my feet hurt," Sierra stated.

She gazed upon the ramshackle platform. Each step we took the wooden floor boards creaked and little black spiders crawl out of the cracks. We started to hike up the abandon trail. The trail hiked up the steep ridges of the Blue Ridge mountain range. Twists and turns we took as we climbed the creepy, yet satisfying trail. Up ahead we saw our first rest stop in hours.

We rested at the water mill up in the heart of the forest. The sunlight shined through the old glass window up on the tower. Adam was looking through his plan while he was sitting on top of the old wooden gears of the wheel. Sierra was playing with her hair, staring out the window. Devon was bored as usual, playing with his handheld. I was for one waiting until everyone gets ready to continue the hunt. Eventually they were ready; we headed out into the cold air. The thick forest atmosphere surrounded us as we hiked up the treacherous trail up the mountain. We climbed the rocky pathway. Every time we climbed a foot the air got colder and colder, well at least when looked down every time we took a step up. The branches of the trees got stiffer and stiffer when we climbed higher to the top. The leaves of the trail were hardened and gentle crunches echoed faintly around the area. Ahead, I saw something moving in the shadows. "Hold on," Adam whispered.

"What is it?" I asked.

"Something is hiding behind those logs," Adam lisped. "Walk slowly."

One by one we crunched on the dry leaves. Slowly we approached the pile of logs. Devon got his baseball bat ready, Sierra had her stance ready and fists too, I began walking towards the log. We jumped over the logs to find a squirrel just collecting some acorns. "Why you got us all paranoid for a squirrel?" I asked angrily.

"Let's not have this conversation again," Adam replied back sternly.

When all of us turned around we all jumped to see someone was behind us with a hiking backpack. "Gah!" Devon jumped.

"Hey hey!" Adam yelled. "It's just Adam Wales."

Adam Wales was one of Adam's many friends, this one was as geeky as he is but more outdoorsy. He was taller than me, short curly brown hair, almost in contrast to Adam's straight dirty blonde. "Whoa!" Wales yelled, "Easy friendly fire, friendly fire!"

"What are you doing here?" Devon asked.

"Hiking?" he asked backed curiously. "What are *you* doing here?"

There was a moment of silence where Devon was staring at him with a blank face. Devon held his bat like a cane and leaned against it and tried to act all cool. "Um the same, but on the extreme side with uh," he paused and looked at his bat quickly and him, "bats."

Sierra sighed, "We are doing, well there is some commotion with The Academy and we are here to stop it."

"You mean the massive transfer?" Wales asked. "I know they sent us a letter about it."

"I don't know if we will be moving to another Academy in that case," Devon stated.

"Let alone leave this campus," I added.

"Then how are they going to remodel it?" Wales asked.

Adam stepped forward and proceeded to explain to Wales about the plot that was a foot. Both of them sat on the logs while the rest of us were leaning against the tree waiting for Adam to finish his very long explanation of the conspiracy. Harley was looking for oddly shaped rocks at the moment. Adam continued to talk to Adam; he was waving his hands around his head and doing these outrageous movements with his hand as if he was telling a puppet story after drinking sixteen cups of coffee. Adam was there nodding his head, and gasping and rubbing his chin as if he had a beard. It was another hour, Sierra, Devon, Harley, Scotty and I were sitting around the tree, our back to the trunk, I was dozing off when Adam came up and cheered, “We have another person to join us!”

“Great, we might be late, ore just cutting it close with the time,” I mumbled.

“That’s right,” Adam gasped. “Let’s go.”

He marched off with Wales heading down the trail. “Remind me to punch him next time he does that,” I groaned to Sierra.

“Will do,” grunted Sierra.

We all got up and quickly ran to Adam and Wales as they were already down the trail.

“By any chance you saw something while you were hiking?” Devon asked.

“In the forest?” Wales queried. “Yeah, somewhat up at the dam up stream.”

“What stream?” Sierra asked.

“The aqueduct river,” I explained. “It runs from the mountains and into an aqueduct that runs over the branch line, then through a river that feeds into our water supply, the lake at the bottom of the complex.”

Wales nodded. “Yeah, there's a dam near here.” he added. “I saw two semi's leaving a depot a quarter-of-a-mile from the dam.”

“Come with us,” I replied. “We might need you.”

We continued our journey upward to the cold river. We reached the edge of the forest or in other words the bank of the river. The dam was nothing but a low dam with brown concrete walls and buildings with dim yellow lights shining through the windows on top.

"Let's get close," Devon replied.

"Are you sure?" I asked.

"Yeah, what if they are guards in the next ten meters?" Adam asked.

Devon glazed at us with focus. "Then we take a chance," he lisped.

He jogged along the shoreline of the river; we followed him all the way to the edge of the dam. Water rushed through the opening. A long metal grid cross the bottom span of the dam, a metal fence was running the length of the dam on the other side of the grid. Devon gentle set his foot on the grid. Faintly you could hear the creaking of the grid. "Devon is not safe," Sierra pointed out.

"So what?" he spiked. "I'm willing to take a chance."

"Like what you almost did to Wales back there?" Scotty asked.

"Something like that," Devon replied.

All of us stepped onto the unstable grid. When we were about fifteen meters in, the grid started to tip over towards the river. We looked below and saw the sharp rock that the dam was sleeping on. The whole platform jerked down; some bolts, screws and supporter beams fell into the rapid below. "Devon! Damn your weight!" Scotty yelled.

"Shut up!" He yelled. "It was old any weight would of done that."

I found a ladder and a concrete platform with a steel door on it. "Guys!" I yelled. "Up here!"

The metal platform jerked closer to the rushing death rapids. More and more parts fell into the white speedy rapids. Tension began to rise. The horrid creaking of steel and rock became louder and louder every second. The platform finally split into two; black steel poles tumbled around the roaring rapids. Devon and I were on the dam side, while Wales, Sierra, Adam, Scotty and Harley were on the other. The other side was dropping and tilting towards the death spelled rapids. "You're awfully quiet," Adam asked Scotty.

"I'm thinking," Scotty replied.

"Jump!" I yelled.

And all of them did, except Adam. He held onto the edge for his dear life. "Crud! Help me here!" he yelled.

I grabbed his and haul his sorry behind up here. "Crud, thanks," he shivered.

I patted him on the back. "Nothing to worry loser," I panted.

We were well in our way inside the dam. Inside, rows of pipes covered the ceiling, gauges and pipes covered across the walls. It was like the corridor I ventured through to the Vault where I met Cornelius, but with less gears. Steam hissed out of the cracks of the pipe joints. The dim old-fashioned light bulbs flickered as the electricity raged down the copper wires. Sparks flew from various electrical junctions near to the brown-greyish pipes. Cautiously we walked into the corridor covered with pipes, gauges, copper wires with clear plastic coverings. We came to an intersection; a huge dim bulb hanged in the middle of the hallway. Water dripped from the huge aged white pipe above us. The sound of rapid electrical buzzing grew louder as we went to the left. "Hear that?" I paused. "Something is ahead."

"Must be the motors," Adam replied.

We hustled towards the sound. Every meter we ran, the loud sound became an earsplitting screeching nightmare. We came across a huge room were the pipes and wires separate and connect to the four mammoth-size generators from the early days of electricity. You could see the bright flashes of sparks in the rotator part of the generator; along the concrete walls was a row of transformers collecting the precious power from the generators. We went down the stairs gazing upon the massive modern marvel. “Holy crud,” murmured Wales.

I looked down and saw the rushing of water turning the large turbines. “What’s this all for?” Devon asked.

“Beats me,” I replied.

We continued our journey around the large brown generators. The magnets were a blur when we pass by them. The sparks jumped to different places as it turned in mind-spinning speeds. We reached the other side of the room and found the control room to this power room. Our hairs were standing up as we reached the stairs. In the room, we saw the whole picture. The circuit board was glowing brightly, all of the rusty power switches was repaired. “What the hell?” Wales exclaimed. “This power station wasn't used in decades, seems like someone just powered it up.”

“Why?” Adam asked.

Then, out of the blue, the alarm went off. “Crud!” I exclaimed. “They found us!”

“Easy!” I hissed. “They are just opening something, hear that?”

I heard dull thumps echoing from further down the corridor. I looked around the dimly lighted hallway. I also examined the rustic wooden wagons. “I don't know,” I paused. “But there’s bound to be an exit down there.”

“So how are we going to move?” Sierra asked.

“We can use those wagons, to move a lot quicker here and to move the Hive project materials and equipment when we find them,” I stated.

I saw there was a corridor that sloped down and heard water pouring in. “The sound came from there and I think it’s slightly flooded. The wagons can be used as boats," I explained. "Grab two, Scotty, Sierra and I are in one, Wales, Adam and Devon the other."

"Why do I have to be with them?" Devon asked.

"To keep Adam in order," I stated.

"Fair enough," Devon shrugged.

"Crud," Adam whispered.

We all got into our wagons and raced down the sloped corridor and splashed into the water, it was slimy and cold. "Didn't see this coming," Sierra stated.

We swam to the cab of the train. All we found are years and years of dust lying on all of the colorful controls. Cobwebs hanged from every nook and cranny in this cab. The floor was covered in grease. The handles were rusted; glass gauges were shattered from the inserting of steel nails. The cab wasn't any different from the corridor, dark and damp. Grease water dripped from the cooling coils on top of the cab. I was shinning the flashlight into the engine compartment trying to find a way to start it up. I could see years of build-up surrounding the early electric motors. No copper wires were contorted, but the only thing blocking the success of starting up the engine was the dust and cobwebs. I wiped some cobwebs off the copper wires, blew dust off the rotary converters. I got up and walked towards the controls. I wiped off every single cobweb and pile of dust off it. I found the reverser handle and pulled. As I did, a creaking sound was coming from the engine compartment. I twisted the engine key and the engine was humming with electric life. I pushed the throttle stiff greasy throttle forward; the engine slowly lapped the greasy, cold, black water. The cab lights flickered on, but it was dim (what did you expect from an aging locomotive?). I looked behind and found flatcars of wooden crates. As we emerged from the dingy tunnel. We were on the other side of the dam. We could see the convoy of semi-trucks lining up on the side of the dam. We went up an incline and stopped at a weighing depot.

The train screeched to a stop in a small dark shed. I started the engine again; we were off going deeper and deeper into the tunnel. Dim orange lights whizzed by the train as we went faster and faster into it. We came to a large room with two tracks and platforms. I looked back to see the end of the track outside on the riverside. "Shoot were coming too fast!" I yelled.

Devon jumped for the brake. He tugged on the rusty handle as it creaked. Adam joined followed by Sierra, Scotty and me. "Pull!" I yelled.

Tension filled the cab, columns of steel and concrete whirled by as we got closer and closer to the rocky ridge. The lights flickered on and off repeatedly; the small black lamb swayed back and forth. The floor rattled with indescribable faith. The old gages shattered as we bump along the two electric rails. The smooth ride of escape became a horrifying roller coaster ride to a watery end. Sparks flew from the lighted controls, cobwebs and dust fell from the roof onto our heads. Heat was building up in the cab. I looked back and found the rubber seals around the engine room door started to melt. The fragrance of burnt rubber filled the small tatterdemalion cab. With tension tightening our spines, we pulled the brake lever, not to mention the handle right of the slot. We fell back as the deafening screech of metal wheels on electrified rails entered our ears. The wagons behind us, were totaled, not to mention our escape hole. The worn wagons zig-zagged in front of the tunnel portal, the portal was sealed with twisted metal and unsound pieces of wood, sticking out of the huge pile of Bauxite. The lights of the cab slowly flickered to its normal position, as in not glint. The smell of the mixed aroma of burnt rubber, sweat and burning electrical components was suffocating our noses. We gaged about the smell. I was about to vomit over the greasy floor until Scotty slammed the door open.

Everyone collapsed onto the cold ashen platform, gasping for fresh air. "God!" I gasped.

"Harley, where are you?" Scotty coughed.

We looked back and found that no one was in the smoking cab. "Cru....We left him behind!" Devon shouted.

"Shoot, they'll find them soon," I replied.

"So if they find them," Adam paused, eyes glazing at the blazing controls, "they'll find us too."

"Then we have to get our behinds going," Sierra replied.

We jumped down on to the gravel. Carefully we stepped over the electric rails, so we won't end up like the train, all fried like burnt hamburgers in the middle of August. At the other side of the room, we came upon a set of rooms filled with nothing but wooden crates of with red letter reading *Electromagnetic Energy of Vortex Generation*. What in the friggin' hell is this squat? Electromagnetic Energy of Vortex Generation? What does that mean, I mean; I know what electromagnetic energy is, but vortex generation? Sierra found another set of crates reading Nitroglycerin Supply Box. That I could understand is a crate filled with dynamite sticks. Devon found in a small storage closet a map of every abandoned mine in the area. The closest one was the one at Carven Caverns, along with that map, were the blueprints for the dam. "Holy crud!" Adam exclaimed. "This is where the Hive is located at!"

"This is the lab?" I asked.

"Yeah!" Adam replied. "This is where the Hive is!"

We heard more clanking from above. "They are here," I sighed. "And they are looking for this."

"Why we came here before them?" Sierra asked.

"They must have come in a different way," I explained. "There must be a rail access close."

"There is," Wales answered. "It wasn't too far from the dam where we entered, it's an abandoned spur line, old factories there hidden in the middle of the forest, well over run by them."

"So they are here," I sighed. "They must be close by, we can chaos."

"How?" Sierra asked.

"Wales what are you training to be at the Academy?" I asked.

"Electrical Engineering, signals and electronics and stuff," he replied.

"Can you redirect the rail traffic to block the train?" I asked.

"Sure why?" he asked.

"I have a feeling we have the equipment here," I smiled.

I went a door behind the crates and opened the door, inside was a large lab, the floor was a grid with underwater lamps below it, the room was a large hexagon, the center was a large column covered with pipes, gauges, windows looking into the inside of the column. The outer walls were covered with benches, with computers, parts of all sorts, mechanical and electronic equipment. "I found it," I gasped.

Chapter 9: Operation
-Same Day-
Afternoon

The chamber was quite large; we saw the words Hive painted on the walls with yellow paint, though now it's all deteriorated. "So this is the lab?" Adam asked.

"This is the Hive, but why is it called the Hive?" I asked.

We began to hear clanking and grinding but not from above but below us. "What's that?" Sierra asked.

Wales and Adam quickly went to the nearest computer terminal and started to find a map of the complex. "Got it!" Adam yelled.

"Put it up on the screen," Wales ordered.

Adam pulled up the Map on the larger screen of the lab. The lights flickered and so did the monitor. It was a large blue print of the complex; it showed the Hexagonal lab connected to underground rooms and vaults with a series of tunnels. There was another set of levels below us, large rooms connected by tunnels that snake underneath the entire Blue Ridge Region. "It's a manufacturing plant also," Scotty pointed out.

"So the Hive is a factory?" Sierra asked.

"No, the Hive is what's being built here, or is building something here," I stated.

"Abercan must of have known and been here and collecting whatever they are building here," Wales added.

"What's being built here?" Adam asked.

"Something that would be effective to wipe us gone along with the Academy," Scotty replied.

"We have to get down there," I ordered. "You guys go to the corridor and find an elevator."

As everyone was coming out of the room I got a message on the PDA. It was from Cornelius. The text read "If you take them, they will know, if you don't nobody will know you and you will be forgotten. Take the hematite hard drive, and the map of the facility." I looked around and saw a lone dark silvery hard drive on top of some blueprints and maps. I grabbed them all and placed them in my messenger bag. I jogged my way of the Lab and opened up the map. "Where do we go?" Scotty asked.

I looked at the map and saw a tunnel that seemed to slope down into the levels below. "There's a tunnel there," I pointed. "It'll lead us to the factory floors; we'll see what they are building here."

We walked down the dirty corridor and felt the tunnel sloping down the suddenly I felt a bump on my head, it was a dead end, but the tunnel seemed to be sloping down still, well at least the ceiling. "Now what?" Adam asked.

We heard cracking below us. "Devon," Adam asked slowly.

"Quit it with that!" Devon snapped

The floor did snap, the ground below us opened up and steam came rushing in, we fell through the factory levels, passing the conveyor belts and pipes until we landed in a large waste material bin. We got up and steam was shooting out of these large half cylinder drums lying horizontal side by side. Pipes covered every square foot of the ceiling. Boxes were being dropped from a stainless steel chute above us. Gears of every kind were spinning around underneath the conveyor belt. Steam engines were spinning the belts at full speed. Electric motors buzzed above our heads as they transferred large silver cylinders of red liquid in them. Large glass silos of the same red liquid poured was sucked out of the silos with large flexible clear plastic tubing. At the same time hot water was being poured in out of from the broad drain tunnels behind us. A glass container with metallic caps on each ends fell from the belt above. The glass shattered into minuscule pieces and the red runny liquid poured upon the hot watery surface. The liquid bubbled as it spread towards us. Huge slimy bubbles began to pop as the rushing current drew it closer to us. Wales gazed upon the liquid as it grew closer towards his exposed hand. With a huge amount of luck, the liquid stopped. The bubbling froze to a complete stop. "What happened?" I asked.

Sierra touched the red solid, it was now wet clay. She was having so much fun molding it into different shapes. We heard a high pitched squealing from above. We looked above and saw a container much like the one that broke being overloaded. The glass broke and flew in different directions but the liquid fell on Wales arm and burned. "CRUD!" he screamed.

The liquid burned his skin. Wales peeled the cooled solid off his skin. He was groaning when he peel off the clay which ripped his top layer of skin. The section that the liquid landed on was now bare-pink. I could imagine how painful it was peeling that, liquid/clay thing hot off your skin. I mean what is it for? Why is there a hidden depot in the mountains? And did we really stop part of the operation. Is there another back up plan in this entire vortex of perplexity? Sierra, Wales and I got up and looked around trying to find another exit. "Which way should we go?" Wales asked.

Sierra and I exchange looks; we didn't have the faintest clue. We hesitated, we called out different answers jarring at each other. "Guys cut it out!" Wales yelled. We need to find a way out of this mess."

Sierra and I again looked at each other, even though we had worked with each other for weeks, we didn't really nailed down constant cooperation just yet, but I sense we will, eventually. "I say we go in the wash tunnel," I murmured.

"No," Sierra disagreed. "We follow the belt."

"Nah-uh!" I ratted.

"Uh-huh!" Sierra claimed.

"Nah-uh!"

"Uh-huh!"

"Nah-uh!"

"Uh-HUH!"

I looked at her and stepped about three steps away from her. I guess she had practice from arguing from a sister or friend. Anyway we headed down underneath the web of piping, wires and gears that lies below the grid ceiling with the dime orange-red light from the lamps fixed at various points. The hallway was not actually a hallway with solid walls, it was much like cages with two sides cut out to make a protective walk way, and I can see why. Scrap pieces banged and smashed against the grid ceiling from conveyor belts above. The pipes rattled with a high pitched ringing, the wires rocked side to side. The gears, well, nothing much happed to them much, they kept on moving 'round and 'round as fast as they could. At almost every bend there is in the piping hot water leaked out and dripped to the concrete floor. Steam hissed out of the cracks of the thick, archaic, dark maroon pipe. The caged walkway creaked every time more and more junk is poured on top of it. What really shivered my bones was the sound of a blade turning at high velocity and some sort of domestic animal dying, hope is not a dog (later on I found out it was a dog, unfortunately). We kept moving on slowly looking at all of the different arrangement of gears, pulleys, belts, pipes, wires, beams, the list goes on. Red lights blinked at every post on the side of the walkway and above us was a large dirty white pipe looming above our heads with cold gases pouring upon us. At one point eh pipe became a large rust box with smaller different colored pipes connecting to the box. On the box were six poles sticking out of the box with gages of different sorts rattling. What kind of operation is this? Is this a factory of bombs? What in the world is Abercan building here?

To our right was a huge clear pipe with chrome rings holding the sections together; the piped was filled a quarter of the way, with wash water being drained from the direction we are headed to. We came upon junction some 20 meters away from the last turn we made. We went up the rustic stairs, still in the protected walkway. We looked at all of the pipes that lie above the bundle of wires and gears. We gazed upon the white rusty one with the gases pouring out from the small lids on top of the pipe. We continued our walk as we climbed more and more staircases. Man it is like a huge factory in here. Ahead of us, partially tucked in the rocky wall, was a bay window with controls lined up against the stone wall. But the walkway ended at an elevator. The elevator looked like it is malformed shape. The scissor type door was jammed open. The walls were bent inwards and outwards at every angle. All three of us got in the elevator tightly. Wales pushed a green button with part of the plastic covering missing. The electric motor droned to a whimsy start. The cables creaked and groaned lifted us to the second level of the complex. There we found a way to get into the control panel. Sierra and I examined the antithetic controls on the panel lined below the windowsill. Wales on the other hand was fast at work hacking into the files on the computer. "Okay our goal is to take anything essential here and take it back to the Academy," I stated. "Meanwhile if you see anything crucial to Abercan and his plans, wreck it."

I turned to Devon holding up his bat. "Devon, any servers that Wales and Adam find that contain Falcon Industries info, take a swing at it, and don't go easy on it, unleash the fury," I added.

"Will do," he nodded.

"Wales, got something," Adam yelled.

Wales and I went over to Adam's terminal and saw that Falcon Industries was creating some sort of armor suit and weapons with the liquids being produced here and The Hive was building it. "Looks like they hacked the Hive and are using everything in here to build what they want, with the help The Hive," Adam explained.

"So the Hive is a computer," I stated.

"A system," Wales corrected. "He's using the Hive because the Hive knows what everything is."

"So what do we do?" Adam asked.

"Corrupt Abercan plans, reroute the rail traffic to block them or cause a train wreck," I ordered. "Meanwhile, I guess we need to find the essential parts."

"They are scattered around here," Wales added.

Then we spotted small shiny crate that fitted like back packs in a large open locker.

"Maybe these are it," Sierra pointed.

"All of us," I yelled, "grab as many as we can carry and let's head out!"

Sierra picked up three crates; they all seemed to connect to each other like interlocking Lego crates. I noticed that all of the crates had the same symbol, a white hexagon printed on them. "These must be The Hive crates," I stated.

"Must be important," Wales added.

"Important enough to not let Abercan get to them," I stated. "Everyone get all the crates, we'll find some wagons to put them in and roll them out of here to the Academy."

"Where are you going to put them?" Sierra asked.

"Out of here," I said.

"No I mean in the Academy," she added. "Where are we going to store them?"

"For now in our rooms, then I'll find a place to put them all in," I answered.

"It better be something secured," Sierra stated. "I mean if Abercan wants it so bad, it better be in some sort of vault."

"Trust me I have an idea to where I'm going to put them," I stated. "But for now I want them out of here."

Everyone scrambled to get them into make-shift wagons and carried them like messenger bags and backpacks. All of them seemed to look like shiny metallic hiking backpacks. Devon was carrying the most he looked like an armed cyborg, he had four on his back, one on each side like a messenger bag. He also had one on each arm like an oversized gauntlet. "I'm Ironman," he growled.

"A bit too hefty," Adam teased.

Devon then swung his arm smacking Adam with the metallic case. "Okay, you're Ironman," he groaned.

He went back to his terminal dragging a crate with him. "More like the hulk," he whispered.

"Say what?" Devon asked.

"Nothing!" Adam quipped. "I'm working that's all, lalalala!

Chapter 10: On The Run
-Same Day-

Two hours has passed by. We didn't stay long in the control panel. Wales and was busy corrupting the plans and setting up a train wreck. The constant clanging of metal rattled my ears. The pipes above us rattled violently. "Listen, Wales could you hurry up?" I asked nervously.

"Why?" he asked.

He turned around and looked up to the pipe shaking. This is not good. We all backed away from the pipe and closed in to the door. The pipe was wrecking the bands that are holding it up. The screw from the band was drilling a larger hole in the ceiling. Cracks started to spread across the rocky ceiling. Steam and hot water shot out from a bend. When things seemed to go downhill, everything fell silent. Steam stopped hissing, water quit dripping, the pipe swayed side to side until it stopped. The room was filled with the muffling of the machinery outside the control panel and in the production floor. It was a short "earthquake" as you might describe it. Sierra, Wales and I exchanged looks eye to eye. Adam ripped the map out from the printer when the printer droned off. "What...was...that?" Sierra gasped.

"Don't know," I lisped.

From out of nowhere, we heard a faint high pitched whistling sound from the ashen box next to the left side of the control panel. The box blew wide open in less of a second. The small hatch flew across the room and stuck into the rocky wall. A huge crack ripped through the wall and up to the pipe, not to mention the floor too! The pipe fell and smashed the controls. Sparks flew away from the pipe during the impact. Another blast of debris destroyed the left side of the panel. Water poured out of the remains of the pipe above our heads.

Electrical sparks zapped though the wreck of the panel. The lights in the room blew out. “Get out of here!” Wales yelled.

We dashed out of the door and into the hallway. My face rubbed against the rocky wall when Sierra was pushed by Wales. We dashed down the hallway. I swear I heard somebody yelled behind us. “There they are! Shoot them down!”

Bullets bounced off the walls as distant footsteps became louder and louder every second of the minute. “Dash for it!” I screamed.

Soon enough we were on the run again, but there's no vents to escape into this time. The red warning lights were flashing and the alarm went off. Every door we pass was shut tight. We came upon another hallway with the walls lined with bawdy steel plates held together with rivets. “The left!” Wales yelled.

We turned left to find ourselves back in the production floor. It took another turn to the right and we headed down the side of the automated room. We pass a dozen pipes with the same liquid sloshing through the tight space. The metallic floor creaked every time our heels slammed against it. I saw the exit up ahead; it was huge door with a conveyor belt with walls on the sides carrying the canisters empty of the red liquid. We jumped into the belt burying ourselves beneath the cold glass and metal containers. We were on our way out of the hidden factory, but the thing we didn't expect was this, there was a drop, a 20 foot drop into a chute with glass breaking off the metal caps. “Holy cra....!” Sierra screamed.

We tumbled down the chute hitting the cold metal walls every time it took a turn. I was the first one to be dumped into the large dumpster of empty broken containers. Apparently I cut myself when I landed on top of the can that goes without saying. Sierra was next, a large blade of glass scraped lengthwise on her left arm. Wales rolled into the dumpster with the twisted metal caps slashing across his chest and neck. “Crap!” I groaned as I tried to get up. We tumbled down the chute hitting the cold metal walls every time it took a turn. I was the first one to be dumped into the large dumpster of empty broken containers. Apparently I cut myself when I landed on top of the can that goes without saying. Sierra was next, a large blade of glass scraped lengthwise on her left arm. Wales rolled into the dumpster with the twisted metal caps slashing across his chest and neck. “Crud!” I groaned as I tried to get up.

A small piece of glass and metal was stuck in a cut on my right leg. My body was submerged beneath the broken cans my foot was caught in large machine with hole in the middle and blades surrounding it. I looked up and saw dim lights flickering and pipes with lights at each band gleaming bright. Suddenly I felt a huge jolt, the cans in front of me began to move towards me. I found out that the dumpster was tilting on one side. We fell again, but this time we grabbed onto a bar next to us. I grabbed the bar with antediluvian chipped yellow paint on it. Wales then tumbled after, then Sierra. Wales grabbed my foot as he was dumped out of the dumpster; my hand slipped on the bar, but yet I still held on. Sierra grabbed Wales's ankle and I lost grip on my left hand. The bar broke off the dingy metal plate that was held by rustic bolts. Now the bar was only hanging on one plate, and this one won't last for long, I can assure you that. I looked down and saw large canal of water. Not only have that by a plethora of pipes dumping watered into this canal. Above us was the same bundle of pipes crossing the span and entering the old steel mill next to us. I looked below at the canal searching for an entrance to the steel mill. I spotted one next to the pile of unused pipes and coils of fresh copper wires. In a second I was thinking should I let go or not?

At the second I was about to let go, the bar did it first. The plate broke in half and we fell in to the cold calm water. We came floating up back to the surface. "God! Friggin' cold!" Sierra shivered.

"No duh," Wales coughed.

"Come on guys," I spitted. "There's a way out!"

We came upon a yellow ladder on the concrete wall. Even though we slipped we still got out of the frigid canal and into the warm mill. We hid in the old boiler room where less activity was occurring. Steam flowed out from the pipes gently. The light above us swayed back and forth constantly. We are at large. We know that there are some sick people now after us because we uncovered their scheme. Speaking of that, we still don't know half of the plan Abercan is unfolding. Where will the liquid be unloaded? And when? We don't really have much time when it comes to finding out and stopping. We didn't spend a lot of time hiding in the small room. Again, the three of us dashed down the cold hallway with the large rusty cranes, hooks and chains dangling above us. The floor vibrated every time our feet slammed against the gridded floor. Bundles of different sizes pipes, wires, junction boxes lie above our heads held up by a steel web of beams. Lamps are place every 5 meters away from each other. We could hear the water gurgling through the rusty steel pipes. Steam gently hissed out from various vales and connections that intertwine with the wires that loop in and out the junction boxes. We came upon a large hallway, the main corridor. Above our heads was the same deal, but with bigger pipes and wires. The web of metal beams stretch across the corridor to the other side. A huge gridded floor lied above the frame. The same deal with the other floors above the second, that is until the fifth floor. In the middle of the corridor was a huge trench with large steel silos with a long glass window, about five feet wide, that goes from the bottom of the silo to the top where catwalks jump from one silo the next. The top of the silo ended up on the fifth floor, being a guess from just looking down from here. On the north side of the complex was the molten buckets lying there alone and chromatic. To the south side was the two railroad tracks that hauled the buckets out of here to the processing plants around the complex. The whole corridor was empty, not a soul, except us, existed in here. The moonlight dimly shone through the skylights way above our heads and the silos. It was silent, only the distant hissing of steam, gurgling of water and the rattling of chains echoed in the vacant mammoth-sized passageway. “Where are we?” Wales asked.

“We are in the main corridor of the factory,” I explained softly. “In other words we are in the production floor.”

“This where they made the steel beams?” Sierra asked.

“Not only beams,” I corrected. “Rails, plates, pipes, cables in different shapes and sizes.”

Wales and Sierra gazed upon the large corridor. “What are those silos for?” Sierra queered.

“Don't know,” I replied. “That’s why we are here, to find out what’s with the silos and the liquid.”

“How's being here gonna solve anything?” Wales asked impatiently.

I looked at the rails on the south side of the passageway. Above it was the bundle of pipes from the silos held up by steel beams along the side of the track. “When we escaped from that...place,” I paused. “I saw the pipe with clouds pouring out coming into here. My best bet is this, the pipe leads to those silos.”

“So where do we find answer?” Sierra asked.

“Follow the rails,” I pointed out.

I started to walk towards to the southern entrance. Wales and Sierra followed with no idea what I just said. Outside were more pipes from the walls of the factory joining with the plethora of pipes above the double track. The pips lead us to a large building with no walls whatsoever. We could see the platforms and beams that held up the floors, vents, pipes, wires, etc. Two large smokestacks rose above the building with their small red lights around the edges blinking every ten seconds. None of the yard lights seems to be working. The complex was cold, bitter and dark for all I can say. Might sounds weird for you, but I kind of liked it for all I care. The tracks made a straight shot underneath the processing plant. When we reached the building, we saw molten iron buckets lined up with their chains cut off from the cranes above the track. We crossed the track and entered the building where the pipes were red hot. Wales leaned against one to rest; he ended up with a scar along his arm. "Crap!" he yelped.

"Just get off and let's go!" I sighed.

Wales was still whimpering about his burned arm. We climbed up the sapless metallic staircase. The railing were ice cold, some pipes had thin sheets of ice around the surface. The air was getting colder, the wind became more louder. The more we climbed the stairs the colder the pipes, railings, anything metallic and the air became. We saw more and more thin layers of ice covering the machinery. The stairs finally stopped around ten stories above the ground. To our right were a door and a hallway with broken pipes, wires, junction boxes and such. Now to our right was the end of the platform. There we could see a straight hundred foot drop to the hard, cold, gravel covered ground. Of course, we took the safe way, through the door. Slowly we walked down the hallway and turned left to the door. On the other side of the door, was nothing but another control panel, this time, is out of date. The panel had nothing but computers from the sixties and power switches where you had a handle and the metal bar and you have to pull it down to turn on the electrical circuit.

Anyway, the machinery was covered in a thin layer of frost, the panel was covered in ice. The vents above us were pouring cold air into the room. "Another panel?" Sierra asked.

"Guess so," I nodded as I took a glance at the ice.

Suddenly, we heard a low rumbling noise from the vent. We could feel a faint shake on the floor. The ice began to crack. "Okay, what's going on?" Wales asked.

Then we could feel warmer air flowing out the vents on the wall. The rumbling became louder. Outside the pipes rattled along with the shattered light bulbs. Outside the room we could see the steam hissing out of the maze of pipes surrounding the smokestack. "What going on?" Sierra asked.

I quickly climbed down the other set of stairs which lead me to the platforms that wrap around the smokestacks. The pipes again rattled and a high-pitched squealing came from the electrical junction box above. I spotted a pipe with little windows between joints. The red liquid was filling the pipe really fast. Another pipe just like it was filling up with gasoline. Another was with oil. Gas, oil and the red liquid was being pumped through the network of pipes in the complex from the underground factory. The ice began to melt, hot water began to pour out form the open ended white pipes. The blots of the floor were coming loose. The skinny, aluminum beams began to pull apart from the rusted bolts."Guys," I orated. "They are pumpin' it."

"Pumping what? "Sierra asked.

"The liquid!" I exclaimed.

A cap from the steam pipe flew across the hall and out the building. "Get out here!" Wales yelled.

We slid down pipes passing every pipe of different size and color. We got on a elevator and cut the cables so we can escape from the explosion. The platform that we just on crashed onto the floor below it and so on, only part of the floors fell while the rest just hanged on there. The old-fashioned computer fell smashing into pieces as it clashes with red hot pipes. Fire burst out of the dark dingy pipe that coils around the smokestack. We were coming in really fast. The ground was coming towards us, wait... that's we are coming toward the ground at dizzy speeds. I pulled the emergency brake. Sparks of bright red and orange flew from the brake pads as it rubbed against the metal beams that made up the shaft. We came at least a foot above the ground when the debris smashed on top of the caged elevator. Hot water spilled from the damaged pipes. The old computer slammed on top of all of the debris, the door swung open that instant. "Oh...my...God," Sierra gasped.

Wales was gasping for air. "What are they doing?" Wales asked.

"Loading the oil cans with the liquid," I replied.

"What oil cans?" Sierra asked.

I just pointed at the diesel depot down the hill. "That the train," Wales gasped. "We gotta stop it."

Suddenly, from behind, we heard a distant scream. "There they are!"

"Yeah, one problem," I added. "We have those numb skulls on our tail."

"What should we do?" he asked.

"Run and shake them off," Sierra replied.

"With what?" he queered.

I looked around and saw another truck, but this time is industrial. "How 'bout a truck?" I suggested.

Sierra and Wales looked at me, then at the large truck underneath the water tower. They smiled with pleasure. "I'm drivin'," Wales replied.

All of us ran to the truck. Sierra and I sat in the passenger seats while Wales started the truck. The engine revved as Wales eyed the wall in front of us. "Hell, no," Sierra gasped.

Bullets showered the back of the truck. “GO!” I screamed.

Wales hit he gas, we flew off, crashed into the wall of crates, then a pyramid of barrels. We took a tight sip around the water towers base. We skidded across the gravel. I got out back and found a crate of aerosol cans unlabeled. I took some, took out a lighter from the parts compartment in the hidden factory. Now you know what I did next, lit some on fire. I threw it at the guard as we swooped by them. The cans totaled the car they were in. I found glass bottles underneath the tarp near to the rags and box of matches. I pulled out of the corks and stuffed the opening with rags. I at least opened fifteen bottles. “What are you doing?” Sierra asked.

“Making ammo!” I yelled.

“Let me help!” Sierra exclaimed in joy.

Another security car was chasing us we we zoomed by the oil refinery. Bullets were shattering the back windows of the cab. Sierra and I ducked down to dodge the the bullets. Sierra and I lit the rags in the bottles and threw them quickly. The bottles blew up in flames as it smashed through the windshield. The cars behind them crashed into the burning SUV. We continued to throw our ammunition at the gunmen. The truck swayed and swerved as we raced through the gravel roads that twists and turns around the industrious buildings. By the time we got back to the water tower, we only had one SUV chasing us. The truck was jolting up and down as we crossed the railroad tracks. We took a perfect sharp right turn into a empty ramshackle warehouse. We hotfooted down the narrow aisle. The side of the truck scraped along the shelves. When we were near the end of the warehouse, the gunmen behind us was shooting at every direction. The bullets went through the aluminum frame. One leg of the shelf gave away, then the whole thing started to lean towards the aisle. Not only the shelf was going down, we didn't even see the ramp in front of us. The truck went flying in the air. Sierra and I didn't hesitate to seize the opportunity; we got a handful of lighted bottles and threw them at the SUV behind. The glass shattered everywhere; flames engulfed the front of the SUV. The hood flew of as it crashed to the door of the warehouse. One bottles actually shattered in the engine. You could even imagine what happened next. A burst of flame shot up into the sky, the SUV was now being barbecued. The windows of the warehouse busted into a million pieces (at least I thought), the warehouse was now on fire. The bright red/orange flames lit the dull industrial park. The building's exterior was all rusty, worn and aging; watermarks ran down from the gutters of the roof. Scrap metal lied everywhere next to the garage that was next to the substation. Wales made a half donut before stopping. Wales was laughing with joy. "Whoa, that was cool! Could we do that again?"

Sierra and I fixed our eyes on him, we gave him a 'hell no' look. He looked back with a surprised face. "Sorry! Geez! Lighten up!"

Sierra and I jumped out of the truck, while Wales tried to open the damaged door. Eventually he did, when Sierra and I was already at the substation. Both of us looked up upon the wires that were buzzing with high intense voltage. We could feel the vibration of the electricity rushing through the wires. The transformer boxes were as rusty as my grandfather's truck. The frame of the whole substation was in poor condition. At every corner it was bent out of shape. It seems like it was ripped out its foundation and was placed on another one poorly. All three of us squeezed through the hole in the gate. As passed through the gate I felt the hairs on the back of my neck stand up. The electrical field was so strong that I could feel the current going through my body. We spotted a poor shack hidden in the corner of the concrete walls. Inside the shack we saw a small glowing screen. When we got closer to the window, the screen was actually a computer screen. I scrambled through the door and sat on the dusty, cobweb infested chair. Quickly I tried to hack into the system of the hidden factory. I found out yet another big discovery. When Wales and Adam were setting up a train wreck for the Abercan's train, there was train coming from Front Royal, an Amtrak inspection train. "Guys did you get a collision course to an Amtrak train?" I asked.

"No, to a northbound freight train," Wales corrected. "Why?

"Nothing," I said. "Let's go and take these crates back to the Academy."

"So what we do about the facility?" Sierra asked. "If it's still functional, Abercan can still comeback and use it."

"We wreck it more," I stated.

"How?" Wales asked.

"I was taught this back when I was in the Academy." I paused for a while. "You could short circuit a current if you put more power into a wire. If the power exceeds the wire's limit. It'll short circuit any electrical item it is plugged or connected to."

"Where are we going to get the power?" Sierra asked.

I just smiled with joy. "The factory. Remember those generators?"

"Yes," Sierra nodded.

"Wales, can you overload the generators, push it well past their generating range?" I asked.

"I can try," Wales nodded.

"Don't try, just do it," I commanded.

"I can do that quicker," Adam protested.

Adam grabbed the laptop from Wales and began hacking away, tunneling through the system trying to find the power controls in the servers. "Got it and it's now being set to overpower the facility," Adam reported.

“Set the program on our command, we just don’t need to blow up now,” I ordered.

“Roger that,” Adam nodded.

“You know I’ve been thinking,” Wales paused. “Every system has a glitch, so the answer to why all this is a big mess should be there and accessible.”

“We could have used that thinking earlier,” Sierra growled

“No time to growl and be angry at each other, let’s find the glitch,” I commanded.

Chapter 11: Final Clue
-Same Day-
Late Afternoon

Few minutes passed by, Sierra was surfing the system to find a glitch. “Damn! I can't find one!” she yelled.

Suddenly I remembered, the PDA! “Found it!” I exclaimed. “Now I just need to send the info to Devon and see what happens.”

Then I search for a way to make a signal delay. Success, you know. We have only ten minutes added. “Guys come on find the info!” I exclaimed.

“Where?” Scotty asked.

“We are going back to the facility. See if we are going find more clues there,” I replied.

I dashed down the stairs just to find two guards were coming up. I immediately ran back up the stairs to the control room. “Guys jump out the window,” I panted.

“What are you crazy?” Wales exclaimed.

“Two guards are coming,” I added.

Suddenly everyone scrambled to the window. Scotty got stuck when he attempted to jump out. Behind our backs, we found the two guards standing there at the doorway. One had a battery stick the other had his gun out ready to shoot us. The guard started to attack us aggressively. Bullets shattered the glass objects on the shelf. All of us started to pick up random objects and threw them at the guards. I picked up the chair and threw it at the guard with the gun. Scotty threw a snow globe to the same one. The globe broke into pieces; water spilled on his bald head. “Get the fat girl!” he yelled.

“One with the thighs?” the other responded.

Sierra got really ticked off at that particular moment. “Scotty! Give me that iron,” she growled.

“Why?” Scotty asked.

"Give me it!" she yelled.

Scotty passed her the iron and she threw it with all her might. The guard with the gun flew back with the mark of the old iron on his forehead. It was bleeding but not that much (damn it.) the second guard came charging after us swinging his stick and smacked Wales on his head. A red mark swiped across his face. His infuriated eyes gazed upon him. He grabbed the shelf, with all his might; he swung the shelf like a baseball bat. The edge of the wooden shelf struck the guard's mouth. Wales battered him so hard that you could see the spit and blood fly out of his mouth; to me that was cool and life saving at the same time. The guard fell to the ground with his hands over his mouth. For extra, Sierra ran and kicked him the sensitive spot (if you know what I mean.) All of us ran out the door, down the stairs and dashed across the tracks. We reached the gravel cliffs and did not hesitate to climb up the rocky wall. Bullets chipped off large fragments of rocky of the wall. We scrambled to the
top of the cliff. When we did, it was a straight shot from here and on. The mill was just on the other side of the drain canal.

I was leading the pack to the mill. We stomped on the old metal bridge with dull yellow paint peeling off the surface of the railings. The mill stood tall and dark as we ran into the production floor. The cranes hanged there solemnly and rusted above us. We ran up the metal stairs dodging ever shot that was made at us. The metal rang in a high pitch that pierced my inner ear. Glass from the offices shattered as the bullets zoomed in front of us. I took a left and ran down the aisle. The others were on the other side of the mill. In front of me I saw a huge gap between the two platforms. Below was a straight drop to the cold, hard, concrete floor. I backed up and ran as fast as I could (and that's really fast.) the edge was coming up fast. I took one foot forward and jumped towards the chain in the middle. I swung the whole way over there. The wind was rushing through my hair. I heard a screeching noise from above. I looked up to the crane; the hook was about to give away. The chain fell but the small hooked grabbed the holes of the metal platform. I quickly climbed to the top of the chain, the platform was also giving in. I pulled myself up to the greasy catwalk. My shoes slipped as I ran down the walk, the platform gave away, but yet still hanged from the main catwalk. A shower of bullets was still being shot, the large production floor was now fill with the rattling sound of metal ringing, glass shattering and yelling of different words. I joined the pack again hiding behind the large metal boxes and barrels. We hid in a room that was filled with pipes, wires and new age computers this time. The guards ran pas the room without noticing our voices. "Where are we?" Scotty asked.

"Another control room, or a Data room," Wales replied.

"Is this were the final clue is?" Sierra asked.

"I don't know," I replied. "But one way to find out is to search the place."

All four of us searched the large Data Room. Disk after disk we searched every file that will give us the vulnerability of Abercan plan. Wales was searching on the mainframe when I found a disk that contains all of the details of the plan. "Finding the clue," I hurried.

She just grabbed her PDA and gave me my own. "Where did you get it?" I queried.

"Found it at the computer here," she replied.

"What is it?" I asked.

"A testing facility, The Academy, he wants the Academy to be a testing facility, something about potential of human strength and mind at power for military applications!" Sierra exclaimed. "He wants this place because of us."

“He won’t because of us,” I stated.

“We’re not going to be guinea pigs,” Wales stated. “We’re smarter than that.”

“You know that gives me an idea,” I declared. “Let’s confuse Abercan.”

“How?” Wales asked.

“Well every tank out there has a senor that tells you if it's full,” I paused. “So we set the full sensors to empty and the empty to full. So after that we shut down the pumps and gather all of the information from the database, and use it against him.”

Everyone gasped in surprise. “So we use his wits against him?” Wales replied.

“That’s right,” I answered.

“When do we start?” Scotty asked.

“We start when we find the main power core,” I added.

“Where is that?” he asked.

“In the factory,” I smiled.

“We're goin' back there!?” Wales exclaimed.

“If it our only hope to shut down this mess,” I sighed.

“What if we don't?” Sierra implied.

“Either way the end will be the same,” I paused in grief, “But one way will take us up even higher, and maybe that road will end up somewhere a bit more relaxing.”

“Is that a yes?” groaned Scotty?

“What do you think shrimp?” I asked.

“Yeah?” questioned Scotty.

“Then you have your answer,” I replied. “Come on gang, we have a lot of work to do.”

Slowly we opened the door and dashed out running like hell. The guards from below spotted us and it was the battle all over again. We dashed across the catwalk to the main pipes that were coming from the factory. I stopped and slowly walked on top of it. The others soon followed when I was stepping on the fixed hatch on the pipe. The cold air poured upon me when I walked underneath the coolant machine above. I looked below and saw the pile of scrap metal and the cold canal below. It felt like that my stomach jumped into my throat. "Guys, for you sakes," I gulped, "Do not look down."

Apparently they did. Scotty gazed down and lost his balance and fell but caught on to another pip below us with a catwalk. "Are ya all right?" I yelled.

"Maybe!" he yelled back.

We continued the daring walk over the concrete drop. Soon ahead of us the platform to the factory was clear as water. When all things seem to be in reach it wasn't, I slipped in the red liquid and banged my head on the pipe and fell down to the lower platform. Sadly I kicked Sierra's foot and she fell too, along with Wales. First I slammed against the floor, then Sierra on top of me, then Wales. God was that painful. We got up and saw not one but three entrances to the factory. "Okay which way is to the generators?" Wales asked.

"Just follow the copper color road to the magical land," I replied sarcastically.

"What copper road?" Scotty asked.

I just gave him a dull and pissed look at him. "What? What? Wha...oh," Scotty sighed.

"Just follow the power wires to the generator," I sighed.

I turned away from Scotty and went to the door to the left. Inside was a long dull hallway with sparks flying from various small wires; the main one above us had green lights glowing dimly around the casing. The tunnel was moist and smelled like Devon's jacket after a run in the summer. Yeah, that bad. After a hundred feet, we came to yet another junction but with two ways. One to the right where is pitch black and the other one where the water drips from the walls and the ceiling.

Either way the wires both split, but one way was lit, the water way. "This doesn't look good," Wales replied.

"No duh," I sighed. "But it's the only way to the generators."

The deeper we got into the hall, the higher the water level became. It went up to our ankles, then halfway to the knee. Then the tunnel became darker and darker as we took a step closer to the rushing sound of water. "Where is that sound coming from?" Sierra asked.

"I don't knoooooow!" I yelled.

Water came rushing down to a large drain pipe. A dull regular light was beaming dully out from the pipe. Wales and Scotty tried to hold on but they didn't of course. Sierra slipped, but I grabbed onto her hands. My shoe lace was stuck on a broken pipe; I could feel the pull of the current ripping my lace. "Hold on!" I yelled.

The lace snapped into two, Sierra and I fell together riding the current down. It was just like those rides at the water park where you go up in a tower and slide down in a tube to the bottom with water rushing and pushing you. I tell you it was fun that is until the end. The drain pipe joined another pipe with more water rushing out. The current pushed us faster and faster. The water was getting deeper and deeper and colder by the second. We found a raft out of wood, aluminum tiles and plastic. Apparently it was strong enough to hold our weight on it. The tunnel became broader and taller as were went farther down the raving rapids. We crashed onto a dry pipe where the sound of electricity was buzzing. We followed the sound and we found the source, the large generators. We saw the large grimy green generators producing immense amount of electricity. We stood behind the gridiron looking at the large facility. We saw next to the gridiron on the other side was the large power wire from the steel mill. The problem now is how do we get to the other side of the gridiron? I looked around to find an opening that will lead us to the generators. I tripped when I started to walk back to the rushing underground river. I found a manhole embedded in the concrete. “Sierra, look here!” I exclaimed.

“What is it?” she asked.

“Is the entrance to the generators,” I answered as I tried to lift it.

Sierra helped lifting the covering off the hole. We threw the covering away and the tunnel echoed with the deep ringing of the iron manhole covering. We slid down the hole to see ourselves at an outlet. The generators were located on large metal and wooden platforms on the other side of the sea of green grimy water. “Now how the hell are we going to get over there?” Sierra asked.

I looked around and spotted a bridge far to the left.

“There's a bridge, come on!” I exclaimed.

I pulled Sierra as we splashed on top of the man made waterfall. We slipped and slid on the green grime that stuck to the light brown concrete. We ran over the weak wooden bridge to the platform. The large generator was the same kind over at the dam, big, green and rusty. On top of the generators was control terminals connected to each other with catwalks. Around the generators on the ends were stairs that wrap around the generators that leads to the catwalks. No one was in sight, the whole place was empty. I took another good glance at eh place and found out that it was an warehouse partly covered by the mountains. Abercan has dug the floor out and deepen it and access the drain tunnels to bring in water to power up the generators. So now, he used the dam to store his items and stole the plans for the generators. Below I could see the same type of turbines over at the dam. Bubbles of green slime was coming the surface above the rapid rotating of the turbines. The sound of the buzzing electricity was softer than I expected. I guess Abercan didn't access the power settings, thanks to us, we shut down the main terminals so he has to do it manually and we are the only ones who can access it. Not bad for an engineer you think?

Anyway we found no main controls when we climbed to the top of the generators, time was ticking away. The terminals up here were just power gages and condition journals. "Where are the friggin' controls?" I lisped.

"Up there," Sierra pointed. "Over at the main generator controls."

We quickly ran up to the small room with the bay window looking over the generator floor. We found the main terminal covered with dust and Coca Cola syrup on the buttons. The sound of the turbines in was submerged by the noise of the computers processing the information (or as my dad would have called it, the "thinking" of the computers.) We plugged into the system and shutdown the generators, or at least we thought. The generator became to scream with electricity; the turbines spun faster and faster. Water sloshed on to the platform. More and more water was being pulled in. the turbines was now also a pump. Hundreds of gallons of water began to flood the floor. The alarm didn't go off. We ran out of there before some real damage began. The water level began to rise rapidly. Pipes bolted to the walls began to burst cracks and spew cold, slimy water. Time was running out faster than before, we ran out of the floor and into the massive maze of tunnels underneath the complex. We found Scotty and Wales running down the stairs. "Guys up here!" I yelled.

"What are you doing?" Wales exclaimed.

"Wha?" I replied.

"The trains leaving soon!" Scotty yelled.

Sierra and I dashed out of the hallway and down the stairs to race to the train before anything bad could happen or just set a domino effect. We dashed down the wet tunnels; lights flickered as the ceiling of the tunnels started to shake. Pipes burst shooting jets of hot, cold, slimy water out. Gauges rattled like in the cab during an express run; they burst too, ejecting small sharp fragments of glass everywhere. I guess we override the system, but in a bad way for both sides. It was a race to get out of the factory. We returned to the production floor to see over flow of the red liquid oozing through the cracks of the pipes. Steam hissed out from the air compressors on the other side of the floor, the glass containers began to clog the conveyor belt chute. Every electrical component was going whack. The cranes were going back and forth picking up machines bolted to the floor or connected to a power outlet. The vents spewed toxic gas, the fans were spinning out of control. The air conditioning became a huge vacuum cleaner. The papers from the control room was being sucked up by the vents and shredded by the fans (or tacky saw blades if you ask me.).

"What the friggin' hell happened!" I exclaimed.

"Scotty was messing with the system!" Wales blurted.

"Nah-uh!" argued Scotty.

"Wait," I paused. "You can control the factory wireless?"

Scotty just glared at me, gave me a confirmed nod. "You know we could of use that thinking earlier." I groaned.

"Sorry!" Scotty replied. "I was playing games on it!"

"Stop! Now let's get our ass out of here!" I yelled.

Suddenly the factory began to fall apart. Chemical silos began to burst due to buildup of pressure. Pipes crippled to small bars. Vent tunnels fell from their support beams. The whole frame of the underground building was being compressed. Sparks flew from here and there. Hot steam hissed out of pressurized glass silos. Steel structure beams fell from the ceiling and crushed the machines below. Fragments of metal plates flew from one side of the floor to the other. Water spilled from the supply pipes, bulbs fell from their sockets and cause large bright flashes of light. The fluorescent lights at the chemical silos were being shot at by the bolts from the pressurized tanks. The bolt shot one of the lights; a huge flash came after that impact, a loud explosion ripped our ears. The flywheels of the air compressor flew out form their fixtures. One of the flywheels shot out and lodged itself in the rock. From that moment I knew it was time to get out there. “Guys! Come on, go, go!” I yelled.

More rubble flew everywhere; the stalagmites began to fall from the ceiling of the cave. They pierced through the steel oxygen tanks, destroyed the remains of the machines. We dashed out crossing the span of the cave on the entrance. The pipe carrying the liquid was disconnected and fell to the canal below with the liquid still pouring out. A group of guard with their guns at ready point came out form the door on the other side. “Over there!” one of guards yelled.

They shot at us and chased us down the staircases. I pulled out containers with the liquid still inside. I pulled the plug of the top and threw it above. Within thirty seconds, a huge fiery explosion flashed in the early morning light. The platforms above fell to the rocky foot hills of the mountains. All four of us saw the destruction of the liquid. “Come on guys we can't let that happen!” I yelled. We reached the train just to see more guards. “Crud,” I lisped. “We don't have guns.”

“I can make one,” Scotty replied.

“You can?” I asked. “How?”

"An air gun," he answered. "You can launch those things out there."

"Like a grenade launcher?" I replied curiously.

He gave me a confirm nod as usual. Scotty began to search for a pipe and a small air compressor from the rubble of the fight few minutes ago. He found one and a handle. He shoved it together in no time at all. I can't believe what I just saw. I didn't really know that Scotty could do something like this is minutes!

"Here," Scotty sighed as he stood up wiping his hands on his jeans. "That should kick their butt."

I held it and looked at it. "Come on," I commanded. "We are burning up time."

Slowly, we progressed forward hiding behind the wrecked freight cars. We saw the train getting ready to leave the fueling depot. The large pipes were being removed manually. The caps of the oil cans were shut manually also. When the guards were doing all the dirty work, we tucked into one of the back cars in front of the caboose, the private car. The private car was aging quickly, ramshackle and dirty. Dust was spread everywhere; the once beautifully, handcrafted, velvet cushions were sitting there, ripped, aged and stained. The walls were brown and gray, once used to be fine red oak. The windows were all boarded up; everything in this private car was torn and destroyed. A beautiful railroad artifact, a Pullman private car, lies in ruins. We hid beneath the broken wooden seat in the car.

The train jerked forward a little, we knew we were moving on. Beneath the faint droning of the diesel engines, we heard like a motor turning on, an electric motor. I got up and search of the source. I found a small "ancient" motor in of all the places, the bathroom stall. The drive belt was sipping furiously; the drive pole of the motor was already greased. The grease was new, someone else is in here, and it ain't on our side. The private car rattled as the train took up more speed outside the industrial park. Time was running short, we had a mission to do, and we need to do it fast. Scotty was staring at the door with his eyes filled with anxiety. He was looking at a silhouette of a figure fairly tall and skinny. His hair was tied into a pony tail. “Guys someone is at the back platform,” he lisped.

Everyone fixed their eyes on the back door. The figure was walking back and forth, back and forth. Another figure came up to that pacing shadow. The tall pony tailed one grabbed the other on by his neck and threw him off the train. We heard what I believed the bones cracking as he fell upon the footplate and break wheel. Other figs came into the scene, three actually. They all stood up straight, the pony tailed one held the gun to all of them, and they all nodded without fear. Then, finally we could hear the voice of that figure there. It was raspy, filled with anger, and just pure cruelty wrapped around it to top it off. We all knew, Abercan was out there, just six yards away from us. I couldn't believe it.

Chapter 12: Escape
-Same Day-
5:10:47 AM

I just can't really process it in my head. I looked towards Sierra across the dusty aisle. “Sierra!” I lisped. “We head to the other door!”

She nodded and crawled towards the door. “Everyone,” I whispered. “Come on.”

Everyone followed us to the beaten door. We slowly opened the lock and pry the door open. A faint mouse-like squeak caught the attention of Abercan. The lock on his door was jingling, he stepped back and started to shoot at the knob. He slammed the door open, a loud thunder-like boom rattled throughout the dusty car. He looked down at us. He came closer, step by step. His face was revealed, dirty, cuts everywhere, eyes burning with madness. He stood well above us, wearing nothing but black and red. He wore but a beat up, long, black jacket with red fabric inside. His hands were covered by black leather gloves holding a gun and a knife. We were terrified to see his face. As he took another step closer to us, we saw the detail of his horrid face. Wrinkled, a shaved beard, eyes blazing with rage, scars up and down his face. The gray hair was nothing I ever seen before, nice and thick. “We'll this Crew 35 I have been hearing about,” he smiled.

“Oh, crud,” I whispered.

“My one of the best from The Academy trying to stop them,” he laughed. “Guinea pigs of mine soon, and the best too. Well you will enjoy the tests I'll put you through, consider them as puzzles or brain busters to be exact.”

“What's wrong with you?” Sierra blurted.

“Nothing is wrong,” Abercan explained. “I just want to further technology and society; we have the tools to do so but you seemed be in the way.”

"You're insane Abercan," I protested. "The Academy doesn't have to part of your plan."

He started to laugh. "You still don't know anything about the Academy!" he crackled.

Suddenly Scotty shot a full oil can to the back of Abercan he fell forward. "Come on the train is leaving!" We got up and ran to the other door; gun shoots filled the rotten wall of bullet holes. We climbed on top of the train and saw that we are not too far from Roanoke. The cold wind stung our faces. "What are we gonna do!" Scotty panicked.

"Sabotage the train so that it'll crash, breaking the detonator," I explained. "When all done, everyone jumps onto the Black Bullet, we set the brakes, so the chain we hooked up will pull the brake hose and jerk the journal out of the axle box."

"Complex, but efficient," Wales nodded.

"How do we get rid of the liquid first?" Sierra asked.

"We drain it by the valves underneath the tanks," I explicated.

"Underneath!" Scotty exclaimed.

"Not necessarily," I corrected. "More on the edge, though."

"All right," Wales replied. "Let's get started."

"Just be careful, guys," I informed. "One slip and it's your life."

We all jumped to the Oil cans (tank cars); each of us had a tank to take care of. So we drained four cars at the time; we had at least 62 cars left. The train swayed left to right, trying to throw us off. I holding on to the safety bars as the ballast zipped right below me. I broke of the red valve as the liquid gushed out the pipe and onto the cold rocky ground. A loud hissing sound ripped my ears as the liquid poured out. By the time we were at the fifth car, time was running short. Guards at both ends aimed and started to shoot us. Some missed and punctured the pipes, thus helping us (I think.) “Guys, we are running out of time!” Wales yelled.

“Where's Devon?” I asked.

“I called him!” Scotty replied. “He's coming!”

Then, like in the movies, our vehicle came in. *Black Bullet* raced down the other track keeping pace with the diesel, and it was Mac on the controls. “Wales, finish up!” I yelled.

“Guys!” Devon yelled. “Get you butts in here!”

“Get in!” Mac yelled.

Adam threw the chain to the axle box. The hook wrapped around the spring box where the bearing caps are. One by one, Sierra, Scotty and I climbed on board the *Black Bullet*. Sierra and I was on board, when we saw the station limits. “Scotty quickly!” I yelled.

“Where the hell is Wales?” Sierra asked.

Wales was in pickle in this moment. He was stuck on top of the diesel waiting for the Black Bullet to arrive up front. The tension in all of us rose to new levels. This is truly an adventure, not the kinds that you want to experience day after day, but he ones if you want the glory at the end. The rail lines became brighter as we got closer to the yard. I was stilled looking at Wales. “Guys stay here,” I replied. “I'm goin' in.”

I swung back to the freight train to help Wales out. Slowly I climbed to the top of the cold black tank cars. Step by step, I took slowly to reach the engine. At every gap I backed up and ran for my life then jumped to land on the other tank car. I reached Wales in no time at all. His foot was caught in the grill over the cooling fans. I tugged as hard as I can without losing balance thus falling off the train and sending me to the hospital. Time was running out, the station platforms were at sight. Yard lights along the side of the tracks whipped by as the train got faster and faster. One final tug, Wales' foot was out, but the grill was bent big time.

We hurried back to the *Black Bullet*, when we saw Abercan running towards us with a hunting knife. Wales swung over to the train and landed on the side of the tender. He held onto a safety bar, as for me, I swear i felt Abercan's cold breathing down my neck, so as instinct I jumped off but landed on the side of the cab and climbed up. I didn't know Abercan was behind me. I turned around and saw him one foot away from me; so in other words I was one foot away from my death. At the corner of my eye I saw Sierra about to pull the whistle cord, slowly I moved away from the whistle. Abercan was enjoying his battle with me. "You can't win, you bastard," he snarled. "You have nothing but your bones to beat me when I have a knife to slice your sorry excuse for a face."

"Well there are alternatives," I smiled.

The whistled rattled in my ear, hot steam and smoke blew out from the valve. Abercan was coughing horribly, that's the good news. Then again, the bad news is that he jammed the valve with his steel boots. The smoke and steam cleared instantly. "Have any more tricks?" he roared.

"No just that one," I replied sarcastically.

He began running after me with his knife swing in the cold wind. I stopped at suddenly when I was close to the smokestack. "Dead end," Abercan smiled.

"I'm not going down without a fight," I panted.

"Weak words from a tenderfoot, how sad," he replied grievously.

I fell back as he was about to stab me in the chest. But a chain whipped around his wrist and threw him off balanced. Sierra was there with the chain in her hand. "Mess with him, you mess with mess me too," she yelled.

Abercan did only chuckle. "Determination won't get you through this little girl. Heck I don't really believe in equal treatment. I say females aren't allowed on the rails."

Sierra whipped her chain again but Abercan grab the chain and pulled her down to the grimy boiler. "Girls are weak!" he screamed.

"Shut up!" I yelled.

I picked his knife off his hand and swung it across his neck. I left him a huge red line on the back of his neck; he yelled with his scratched voice. "You little snot nosed-" he screamed.

"Ah, did you your mother ever taught you manners?" I asked tauntingly.

He yelled in anger and tried to grab me and bit me. Sierra got up with the chain and pulled him away. Sadly he got a grip of me and bit me on my neck. The pain was immeasurable; I could fell his teeth sinking into my skin. I could feel the blood rushing down the neck. So I slashed the knife down his face. I left at least three marks on his face running over the eye. I was set free, also was Abercan. Sierra and I ran towards the tender and jumped to the coal pile. Abercan pulled out his gun and started shooting. The station was in clear shot. "Devon now!" I yelled.

He pulled the emergency break with all his might, the train skidded across the rails like never before. The train soon stopped at the platform track. Adam pushed the hatch Abercan was on up as fast as he could. Abercan went flying and landed on the platform. Even though, he kept shooting the tender. Sierra and I jumped out of the tender. Abercan kept shooting us, but every bullet missed us, that are until Sierra got shot. A burn circle was forming around her wound on her right leg. In front of us we saw the runaway train heading towards the city. Also we saw some frighten customers running away from the scene. We haven't escaped from Abercan yet. He got up and chased us again. We ran past him, whipping him with the chain along the way. He yelled, "You can't fight! So die already!"

We kept running up the stairs as the bullets dented the staircases. He was right behind us. Bullets shattered the protective glass panels on the side of the walkway. Passengers ran away from the scene. "Get back here snot brats," he snarled even louder.

"Sierra we need to get rid of him!" I suggested.

"How?" she asked.

"Showdown," I replied.

"With what?" she pointed out.

"Will be at the yard," I answered with a smile. "We are going to have more ammo."

We stopped and turned around. He stopped at least three yards away from us. Face to face, eye to eye, we stared at each other. Sierra pulled out her chain, I pulled out my knife. We could hear the heavy panting of Abercan as he stood there, filled with many unrighteousness acts he had committed. "You know, *children*," he snarled, "I have no patience for such child-like stands."

"We are not children!" I protested.

"And we don't do child-like things," Sierra added. Abercan chuckled deviously. "You don't even stand a chance in this world. You know, I think you are frightened now."

We stood there breathing deeply; my eyes squinted at his demonic face. The distant whistle of the incoming and out coming trains was barely heard. "By now your plan is foiled," I stated.

"Oh is it?" he smiled.

He grabbed a remote from his belt and pressed the black button. Nothing happened. "What did you do?" Sierra yelled.

"I did it," he roared in laughter. "Along with another!"

He pulled out a chain and whipped Sierra to the cold granite/iron railing. Along her side was a thick ruby red cut gushing out blood. Out of nowhere, I yelled at the top of my lungs, “Sierra!”

Abercan whipped his chain to my direction but I dodge the long silver chain. The chain wrapped around the metal pole; I ran as fast as I can towards Abercan and slashed him across his stomach. Sierra got up, still bleeding from the whip. Abercan slashed me down my chest. Sierra punched him at his stomach, but Abercan elbowed her on her mouth. I took a M.O.W. yards stick from from the ground and smashed off the soft tip as I whacked Abercan on the head. Sierra did the same maneuver but at the stomach. Abercan did the same also, but with a metal pole. Second by second, tension grew rapidly in ourselves. I felt more anger as I kept fighting him, just looking him in the eye, made me disgusted of what he done to people around him. When we were about to push him of the stairs, he said to me panting, “Keep fighting me, and you will be just like me soon.”

That just tore me apart. Like him? Me being a madman on the rails who wants everyone to worship me while killing the innocent off? I don't think so. He kept talking to me as we battled closer to the stairs. “If you keep doing this, you will corrupt like me,” Abercan smiled darkly.

“Hell...no...I'm...not,” I grunted.

With one enormous push, Abercan smacked me along my face; I fell on my back as he held the sharp end of the pole to my neck. My heartbeat went higher and higher as the acute point of the pole applied pressure slowly to my neck skin. Abercan laughed as he saw my face yelling, “Crap, he got me!” He gripped the pole with both of his hands. “Now, I'll say this for the last time, you will be like me, no matter what path you take," he growled as the blood dripped from his forehead.

"Yeah, I'll still have my friends to help me out if that ever will occur," I bantered.

"Your hope is most annoying to me," he up braided. "What friends? You call this girlie girl a friend to you? I mean do you ever figure that she might turn on you? That she might leave you like Martha at the Academy?"

My eyes widen, I can't believe what I just heard! Did he really call Sierra a girlie girl? Plus, how the hell he knows about Martha and the Academy? "Who are you calling a slut?" I snapped. "She is not a slut and I trust her, plus how the hell you know about me and Martha during the academy days?"

He chuckled as I spoke with sweat dripping down my cold face. "You trust that slovenly woman?" he laughed. "I know about you and Sally because I was there watching your ever move."

He paused as he took in a breath; Sierra was still battling him, but unfortunately Abercan knocked her out with one swing of the pole. Sierra's head swung the other way as she fell down to the cold granite floor. Her pole fell down the stairs; the clanging of the pole down the stairs echoed in the empty air. "She is from Vegas," he graved, "What do you expect? Her family is abusive, she is a loner, why trust her?"

I growled with much anger building up inside of me. My eyes felt as if they turned red, my head was red hot with thoughts of killing him myself instead. Is like that, a moment when you are really mad at someone and you want to deal with him yourself. Much like that guy that causes trouble to you and always hate and want to punch him in the jaw or better, in the groin. Better yet, rather kick him until he can't feel a spot on his body. That emotion is what is going through me right at that moment. "It doesn't matter," I growled.

"She's a kind hearted girl, she has moral and physical respect for herself and anyone around her."

"What makes you sure of that?" Abercan protested.

"Because she is part of Crew 35....and so am I," I added in.

I kicked him at his knees with all my might. With my rage still burning like a wildfire, I snatch his pole from him and started to kick his butt. I stabbed him in the stomach, smacked him across his face, slammed his neck, and bashed his underarm area. Continuously I kept bashing him, even when he was falling down the stairs. I can tell you this from personal experience; this is no ordinary schoolyard fights or a face-off with some stranger you see every day at work. This is a showdown. I was still filled with anger when Sierra, Dev and Scotty joined the fight. Devon brought the shovel from the tender when Scotty brought a very large wrench. All at once we battered him. We didn't even give him time to defend himself. He was covered with bruises, cuts like us. He was getting his taste of his medicine, and we are making sure of that. Then the unexpected happened. Since we got even closer to the edge of the platform, we were about to pushed him off the rails. Sierra kicked him in the thigh and yelled, "That's for calling me a girlie girl!"

Devon was about to push him off when one of his trains swept him up on the same track that his other train was. "You haven't seen the last of me!" he yelled. "You will all die! Crew 35 will never see the world! You'll never understand anything!"

He left zooming down the line, giving us the finger. Adam and Wales walked up and asked, "Is he gone?"

I turned around and nodded. "Yeah," Sierra paused. "Did the train stopped?"

Wales and Adam just gave us a smile; I was assured that was a definite yes. I smiled in victory. "Abercan, learn," I sighed half-laughing.

"You think the train crashed?" Devon asked.

"Let's go check," I replied.

We hopped onto a speeder and rushed down to the bridge. When we arrived, we found flames blazing and burning any remains of the train. The diesel train in front of us was telescoped into the back of the bomb train. Red flames with a blue core was spread over four tracks. The signals around turned yellow and the four fiery tracks were definitely on red. The system was back up and running, I bet Abercan is there burning in the caboose of his escape train. We cautiously entered the demolished caboose to find he wasn't there. The wooden desk in the caboose was on fire, next to be the escape hatch he used to get out from our trap. We found an envelope far from the fire, hidden in a small cabinet next to the smashed heater. The envelope was open and burnt a little. In the sulfur, a lukewarm envelope was a thick raspberry piece of paper with the words, "There's more to come!" written on it. Devon, Sierra, Scotty, Adam, Wales and I gazed at the letter. Is it for real? Is Abercan going to be back? Is really going to find away to kill us? Devon snatches the paper from my hands and found another small fragment of a paper. Devon gazed at it, the side was burnt and the middle was wet. "Dev, what's that?" I asked.

"Another letter," he accounted.

"What does it say?" Wales asked.

"You don't know anything about The Academy, but what you know it's a start," I read out loud.

Devon lowered the paper and threw in the fire. "He wants you two dead," Adam stated.

Sierra and I gazed at each other eye to eye, we sighed at almost at the same time. Sierra and I held hands but hid it from the others behind our backs. I

opened my mouth to say something, but apparently I didn't. Sierra spoke up, "He doesn't want us dead, and he wants control of us, for his testing project."
A piece of metal suddenly came crashing down from the ceiling. "Guys, let's talk out there," Adam suggested.

"Yeah," Sierra replied. "Let's go and find a safer spot."

All of us jumped out from the burning inferno, outside was the train wreck crews ready at work with the fire department putting out the fire as fast as they can. However, they work at lightning speeds, so, this is just a piece of cake to them, or is it? Devon was talking to Wales, Adam, and Scotty about the conflict we are facing. Sierra and I was trailing them back to the station. "Why Abercan wants The Academy?" Sierra asked.

"I don't know, there's seemed to be more to it than we thought," I sighed.

"But at least we have more time to figure it out," she pointed out.

"True," I nodded.

At the station platform, Dave was waiting for us impatiently. When all five of us were on the platform looked up. We thought we were in a mess of trouble, but his frown turned to a smile. My brain completely fried at that moment. Is much like when you are having a test and you think is going to be long but it ends up to be nothing but fifty or thirty questions instead of a hundred and two. "Vanderbilt is waiting for you guys," he smiled.

"Is it bad?" Adam asked.

"Is just a surprise," Dave proclaimed.

In we went to the nearly empty station, up the glass elevators and down the hallway to Vanderbilt's Office. At the end of the hallway, there it was the red oak door with Vanderbilt's full name pressed onto as brass plate. The door slowly creaked open, Vanderbilt was sitting on his executive chair facing the large window that overlooks the station scenery. “Come and take a chair,” he replied happily.

We all sat on the green Victorian chairs that were place in front of the large desk. The brass chain to his desk lamp swayed back and forth ever so little. The clock up on the wall labeled East Coast Time, revealed all of the gears and rods like the one downstairs in the offices. Vanderbilt's Newton's Cradle was going back and forth like the pendulum of a grandfather clock. Black and white and color photos of railroads, work trains, crews and locomotives covered the wall. His engineering diploma was hanging right in front of our eyes; an engineer from Massachusetts Institution of Technology, also known as M.I.T. His chair swung around and he was smiling. His hands covered our files and he stood up joyfully. “Apparently, I knew you were going to do this,” Mr. Vanderbilt stated. “What I didn't know that you were going to suck information out from him.

“Well we had to sir,” I replied. “That was the only way to get to the core of his plan.”

“Yes,” He added. “We too know that Abercan, or whatever he is called, is quite the troublemaker.”

“You can say that again,” Sierra replied.

“He was the same since I first met him,” Mr. Vanderbilt sighed as he fingered with his fountain pen.

“Yeah, he was the same since you...” Wales paused.

Our mouths literally dropped. Did I hear him correctly? All five of us looked at each other. Is that how Abercan got an easy grip on this company? Because he knew him? Our principal? My brain was officially gone, my head was aching form the questions circling my mind. Boy, what you expected to be a thank you and a praise, turns out to be something that no one thought of. The head, the big cheese of the railroad actually knew the madman who wanted to rape my partner at a personal level? My mind was going, going gone when I heard the words he spilled to us. “Mr. Vanderbilt,” I queried. “How did you knew him?”

“Abercan was a person I kept seeing when I was an engineer for the Norfolk and Western in 1951, we were only 25, I gotten my engineering degree and started to work here. Nathan, was a frequent rider and soon began to be a station clerk. I kept seeing him when I was on my daily runs through Roanoke. I always saw him at the window filing papers and answering calls issuing tickets. But two years later, he began to change, he was my best friend, then he turned to a sick man, obsessed with the machinery around him and uses for war, advances in society. We never talked to each other since and lost contact with each other,” Mr. Vanderbilt explained.

Mr. Vanderbilt sat down on his chair and explained, “Ever Since I became president of the Academy board, we began implement a strong engineering program to young students, before I knew it we had a huge network up and down the east coast and to the west. We became a large pool of talent, something Falcon Industries wanted.”

“He wants it to destroy everything,” Devon replied.

“Probably that's the answer,” Mr. Vanderbilt sighed in disbelief. “He wants progress his way, that’s all.”

“So that's all?” Sierra questioned.

“No,” Mr. Vanderbilt bounced, “I have a promotion for you. Crew 35 along with several crew here are titled under Specialists Crews.”

“Specialists Crews?” Devon implied.

“You have the ability of free range research among yourselves within the boundaries of the Academy, I see that your talents are far beyond what I expected," Mr. Vanderbilt. "Go and have fun, The Academy is your research playground, hope you do a lot of good by the time you graduate."

Chapter 13: Guardians
10/7/03
12:30:57 PM

A week into our new arrangements and we are neck deep in our interests and exhausted. The crates we collected ended being in my hands, neither of the guys wanted them or were remotely curious. Adam was just playing with the software he took from the facility. Sierra was leaning to medical and Devon, well he was just studying to get out and explore his options. So I was left with all the crates we got out of the facility. All the crates were all cluttering in my closet. Every time I was going to change my clothes, they all tumbled down. But this time one of them opened and I saw some shiny equipment strapped inside of the case; I saw several hexagonal plates the same kind that Sally and Cornelius gave me. I got them out and laid them out and I placed two together and heard a click. It was sort of like magnets, but they lit up for a moment, the faint hexagonal grid lines on the surface began to glow blue. "Interesting," I whispered.

I began to open all the other cases and they had the same equipment. I began to tinker with them on my desk. Then I found a hexagon disc, about the thickness of my finger and covered my entire hand. The grooves that made the hexagonal pattern were deeper and had the same glow as the ones I put together. I took out the blueprints I took and started to examine them. I saw that this plate was to be cut but following the grid. I began to poke a hole in the middle of this plate and saw that it was a sandwich, the thin outer layers was a stainless steel plate, the next layer was a hematite layer and the center was some sort of silicone with crystals formed in the middle of the silicone gel, it glowed blue. Then I saw that it needed a special circuit board, in a shape of a hexagon that would have fitted in the hole I just made. I found the board and the components needed to make the board. In the middle of the board, a coil of copper was to be placed. In the inside and outer side of the coil there was supposed to be a thin glass tube to be filled with a gaseous substance of a liquid chemical. The blueprints only specified that it was stored in a glass vile with the label Nect-4R. I found the vile and I began the slow and careful procedure of inserting the liquid in the tube. I researched that I could form it into a gas if the power and heat was high enough emitting from the small crystal power cores in the middle of the coil.

The power cores were special type of batteries that fitted in the inside of the coil. They were arranged to make two hexagons so I placed twelve of them like the dots of the clock. In the center was another coil of copper and a bulb in the shape of a ring. On the outer portion of the hex board I place a rotating locking ring that'll lock it into place with the main hexagon. The locking mechanism was lit by small LED bulbs on top of each screw. As I placed inside of the bigger hexagon, I rotated the locking mechanism; small terminals stuck out and were inserted into the blue transparent gel of the plate. I looked at the blue print and it said to repeat the same thing with the red gel hexagon. I grabbed the other hexagon plate opened a hole in the middle of it and proceeded. But this one had an open board design, sort of like a window. The next sets of instructions were to bolt these two plates together with an insulated board. At the end of all this I had a really thick mechanism, I wasn't too sure about what it does. The control mechanism I placed on the window of the machine, it was rotary style, I turned the metal rim of the view port clockwise one click and the mechanism lit up in the middle white. Then I saw a small light bulb, vacuum tube thingy lit up in the case. "Apparently I built a power supply," I sighed. "But where are you getting your power?"

I went out to get testing machines from the science labs and bringing them to my room, I was careful to not be caught, which was awkward when I walking back to my room. I had a voltmeter, gauss meter, amp meter; basically I had a lot of meters. My room in a short few hours became a miniature lab. Spare coils of wires lying around the floor, meters and testing machines occupied my desk and shelves. An oscilloscope was monitoring and displaying the power pulses that the strange machine was giving out. I had the blueprints of the machine pinned to the wall, I marked and highlighted the strange code, it wasn't in words per say, but in a strange hieroglyphics, not familiar to like the Egyptians. I had papers spread in an unorganized fashion across my desk with deciphering notes, trying to figure out what the writings on the actual blueprints meant. The only things on the blueprints that I could read were the pictorials and the instructions, everything else, the labels and the name of the machine was writing in some sort of code. All I could decipher was a numbering system. Zero was an empty corner, one was a circle with a dot at the corner, and the number system went on as if the circle was divided into a grid of nine squares and the numbers corresponded to a shaded square on the grid within the circle. I got a series of numbers but couldn't tell what it meant: 12211209065735221000. Then I only deciphered some of the other symbols, a capital 'M' with two lines crossing it was an 'N', a circle with an arrowhead, or chevron to be precise pointing to the right was a 'Q'. This code at first glance looked alien to me, but when I was deciphering I began to realize that whoever created these pieces of equipment and machines wanted them to be kept a secret and only a few people to know how to use them. I found clues hidden on the machine parts themselves, they had regular words but some letters replaced with the symbols.

I then looked at the clock and it realized it was well past into the afternoon and it was almost supper time. I turned off the soldering tools and powered down everything. I exited my room and headed to the cafeteria. There I met up with Devon, we had a good meal. He talked about the times when Adam was just Adam and how he slaps him or wrestles him for no reason. I laughed too. "He was really that stupid?" I asked.

"Yeah," Devon nodded. "But the dork means well, he's a good friend."

"Hmm," I nodded.

Sierra then joined us. "Hey, how's class?" I asked.

"Eh," Sierra shrugged. "I'm going to the shop soon, to unwind from the imbeciles."

"Oh, doing what?" I asked.

"Clean, I promised a student mechanic a favor," Sierra replied.

"Let me help then," I offered. "I have nothing else to do."

"Okay," Sierra agreed.

And so we are off to the sheds, I was going to help Sierra with her favor to a friend. We entered the shed and it was a mess from the previous class. Some of the railroad mechanics helped us with the heavier equipment; we just picked up the paper and wrappers, dirty rags and some nuts, bolts, screws, hand tools back to their respective places. We went to the back rooms where they keep all the machinery and tools for the repair of the engines. In the greasy room, there were four rows of long shelves that held bins that contain valves, rods, pins, bolts, wrenches, compressors, pipes, basically parts for every type of steam and diesel engine we have on the roster of going to have. Sierra reached in the blue crate to see the large greasy, brass valve that was lying at the bottom. "God this is warm!" she exclaimed.

"Let me see," I requested.

I held the valve in my bare hands and it was lukewarm. The red rubber coated handle slipped in my hands. I placed it back to the blue crate as we explored more of the parts we have in the storage room. As the intense sounds of the torches, hammers, air guns, the loud humming of the electric motors increased. This is basically where we all keep the spare parts from the scrapped locomotives. In other words, this is the hospital of the railroad. Suddenly a shelf started to shift towards us. It leaned dangerously towards our heads. The bolts on the bottom of the tall steel shelf were giving in. All four rusty bolts bent like as if they were made out of plastic. The shelf soon collapsed but we survived the impact. I covered Sierra as the large air compressor on the sixth shelf then tumbled down. Although the pipes of the compressor scrapped my back, Sierra was safe. Other heavy metal items scattered across the floors. When we got up we found ourselves covered in grease and black soot. I got up with my back acing with pain. My back felt as if an army of red ants started an invasion on the bruised portion of my tender back. I set my hand out as sierra got up, I could hear the cracking of her knees as she got up from the wreckage. Just when we were about to leave, Sierra and I spotted a brass key partially covered in the soot and grime from the other dull oily pipes and valves. I took a closer look to it and found it was a n old fashion key with only the two teeth at the end of the brass stick. The handle of the key was curved and pressed in a Victorian style key end. "Where did that came from?" Sierra asked.

"Probably from the crate," I responded.

"Then why is it clean?" Sierra questioned.

I looked for the answer and found a dirty piece of cloth. "Does that answer your question?" I replied.

She nodded as she rubbed her leg. “What lock it belongs to?” Sierra asked.

“I don't know,” I replied eying the marvelous piece of craftsmanship.

Sierra picked up the piece of oily cloth and found three initials: *JRV*. “*JRV*,” Sierra queered. “Who the hell is that?”

“I don't know,” I restated. “But I think I have a clue.”

I turned around and faced the dusty windows and found someone behind the Maintenance shack with a sniper rifle aimed at us. “Duck down!” I yelled instantly.

Sierra and I hit the floor as the window shattered to a million pieces. The whole wall of glass came crumbling down as the bullet impacted the brick wall behind us. Brick dust shot out from the bullet hole that was made next to the electrical box. Another shot rang in our ears, the mechanics ran in and saw what was going on and alerted the rest. “We have a sniper!” One mechanic yelled.

“We are being shot!” Another yelled.

The alarm went off in only the offices and the roundhouse. The blazing klaxon horn pierced our ears as security guards ran in. but the time five guards came into the storage room, the sniper was long gone, deep in the forests of Roanoke. Sierra and I walked out from the wreckage as the M.O.W. crews came out and started to clean the mess. We stayed most of our day in the shed playing around and acting like, four year olds. Even though the wreckage caught the attention of the community, we still acted like it never happened. Well at least for them, for me is just another story. I still feel the pain and confusion that occurred the past few weeks, the crashes, the clues, the mysteries, everything. When I think about it, the hunt wasn't all that bad, but when you think deeper, you'll see the consequences, it’s not going to occur instantly, is just a long chain reaction. But something still warps me in the inside, Sierra. Heck we started to be like brother and sisters. We fight and get along with each other at the same time. Yeah, my family, I have no clue what so ever. We occasionally write to each other, but the letters are just short and brief. Sierra and I on the other hand, we constantly talk to each other. I guess really the hunt wasn't the search for the villain but the unity of my crew. I know is somewhat of a cliché, but bear with me, these events just starts something from the unusual places. In my head I kept thinking, is it really destiny that brought my new crew together with me? Or was it just pure dumb luck? To my belief, is destiny, I mean, everything happens for a reason, but what's the reason this time? Are we going to become more than the guardians of the rails? Are going to be pulled in global conflicts? I mean it is far fetching, a group of young teens fixing the world? You got to admit it is beyond what we could believe. Then again, we are like that, we are just humans. We live and learn from ourselves and others. It is possible, but if so it is, if that good is possible, could evil be that strong too? As I look to the past events, yes, sadly it is. It could happen again, to my extent of knowledge. Adding on my feelings, it'll happen sooner that we could all think. It could be tomorrow one thinks, or a week later says another. To me, it has already started. Nobody cares, because nobody knows. So I guess we are the new guardians of the world, our world, well The Academy World, the secret world of the Academy with all these weird secret projects with cool gadgets and technology, if we like it or not, it's our destiny. So I think yet.

Chapter 14: Birthday Surprise
10/8/03
01:33:03 PM

Finally it is here, Sierra's Birthday! Adam hidden the cake in the freezer in the office space, Devon got the party balloons from the mechanics whom brought in a table from their workshop. After we got everything arranged, we quickly washed off the grease and the ash from our faces. We waited at the entrance of the shed to surprise her, but she never came. We waited for at least an hour. The seconds hand of the clock on the front wall of the shed ticked away as the candles were being melted away and covering the cake in a thin waxy layer. "She ain't coming isn't she?" Scotty proclaimed.

I looked at the waxy cake, the vanilla and chocolate icing was nearly covered by the blue and black wax of the candles. "And just to think," Adam protested, "I slaved for five hours to make that cake!"

"Well," I added. "It won't taste that great anyway!"

"Shut up," Adam growled.

Devon and I snickered softly so Adam won't hear us then smash our skulls with the wrench he is holding. Ten minutes passed like ten seconds and the candles were completely gone. The flame went out and the sun was still up. "Give up?" Scotty suggested.

"Aye," declared Devon, Adam and I.

We got up and cleaned up the area and packed everything to our rooms. Adam was taking the cake to the refrigerator room in the Dining Hall. I went up to my room to put back the table when I found Sierra looking at the city from the third floor balcony. "Not much of a birthday?" I stated.

Sierra turned around casually. "Yeah," she answered.

"Well, we set up a party for you ages ago!" I complained.

"Sorry," she apologized.

"You know, we a have all day to fool around," I suggested.

She looked upon the table and lifted her head and smiled. "Are you thinking what I am thinking?" she smiled.

"Cart race?" I chuckled.

"On the gardens?" Sierra added.

"Grand and Northern?" I asked.

"And the yard," she replied.

We both jumped out of our seats and ran to the M.O.W. sheds on the manor grounds. We crashed in finding a fleet of green, black, blue carts ready to race around the grounds. Sierra and I jumped into two black carts. With on push of the button, we jetted out of the shed to the woods were the extreme terrain of the race was. The carts took the bumps really well. We raced back up the grade to the gardens where we turned left and right, it was a constant fight between us. At first Sierra was ahead by a foot, and then I was, then she, and so on. We head north to where the old greenhouses were built. We jumped up into the air as we flew from top of the northern garden hill and landed on muddy territory. We round about the greenhouses as we flung mud into the air. Sierra and I were neck to neck, we flew down the hill and onto the gravel path to the yard. We took the northern path where it lead the back of the repair shop. The path twists and turns until we reached the old wooden water tower. From there and on it was nothing but a straight, fine gravel path to the yard. We saw the back of the repair shop closing up as we escape from the thick neck of the woods. The orange and red leaves covered the path which made the carts harder to steer. When the back of the shop was fully visible so was the sharp turn; Sierra pushed me to the wall as we turned. But, she didn't successfully push me all the way; I caught up to her in record time. And saw the return mark, the abandon signal tower. We swung around the rusted steel base and ran straight back to the gardeners shed. It was a closer race, neck to neck, up the gravel hill and trough the lush green lawn until we hit the finish line. When we finished, we didn't know who won and lost, it was very close race. "Who won?" Sierra asked.

"I think you did, by half an inch," I replied.

"Damn," panted Sierra.

"Yeah," I paused. "I think that's enough racing for the next two years."

"So that's your promise?" Sierra replied.

"The race?" I stated. "Yeah, I hope so."

"Yeah," Sierra sighed.

"Anything else?" I asked.

"No, just chill," she shrugged.

"Good," I panted. "Because I'm tired as hell."

Sierra laughed a little as we placed the carts back in the shed so no one will know we even had a race with them! We cleaned them before we locked the doors shut to hide the evidence. We left the shed alone and head back to the entertainment section of the manor. We chilled in the library listening to our music. I pulled up my iPod and started to listen to Linkin Park, while Sierra listens to her bands (God knows who they are!). We chilled for the rest of the afternoon.

Come to think of it, I forgot about the present I made for her. Maybe I forgot about it when I was thinking about the events the blurred right through us. It was nothing really. It was just a friendship necklace, more of a crew necklace. It had a sapphire in the middle of the orb with the number 35 encrusted on it. Probably I'll give it to her when the afternoon dies down and the evening comes. I lied down on the beanie bag was I listened to my songs. As the songs played throughout my head, I can't help the fact that I kept thinking about those events. Maybe those were the events that will change my life, probably I'm under a serious test of life right now and I don't really know it! But I know that things like that are bound to happen to us in our life spans. To some it'll happen when they all ready poses the knowledge to overcome it. Some they experience it when they have no prior knowledge on doing anything in that position. I guess my crew and I are in the middle somewhere; most likely towards the uneducated region, but I think in reality, we are really more into the educated region but not by a whole lot. To come to ponder about, the necklace I got maybe a sign that we are closer as friends. It's wired, but is the truth. We ruin like a family, a dysfunctional one at certain points but besides that we do act like a family, just in a weird, my world kind of way. I guess that's why these things just happen to my life. I think there's more to this academy, maybe a moral fact. Well anyway I'll get that answer when I'm ready for it.

I turned around after I stop thinking about the mind twisting question that the hunt brought up. I saw Sierra fast asleep with her music still on, I quickly ran up to my room to grab my gift for her, when I came back like ten minutes later she was waking up. When she focused her eyes on me, I could see that she fixed her vision on the beige and golden box I had in my hands. "What's that?" she asked.

"A gift," I replied.

"For me?" she asked. "I thought you didn't get anythi-"

"Well you thought wrong," I answered.

She looked at me blankly. "What's in it?" she inquired.

"Take a look," I replied. "I mean it is for you!"

She got up from the chair and grabbed the box. "The box is cold," she noted.

I just remembered on that quote that I left my AC on for the whole time! Gosh, I didn't felt it when I went in there and I didn't turn it off! "Well," I paused. "Go open it before I reach my sixtieth anniversary!"

She looked at me suspicious as she slowly opens the box. Her face was changed instantly when she saw the friendship necklace. "Why are you giving me this?" she asked.

"Well, put it this, it's a promise of protecting each other, watching each other backs," I explained.

"So it's a promise thing?" she implied.

"That and a sign for our, um, friendship," I added.

She nodded as she put it on. "Thanks for the gift, and the day," she smiled. "I haven't had much fun in so long!"

"Well, I'm glad you had fun," I chuckled.

"Yeah," she sighed.

"You really thought I was a sexist?" I blurted.

"Well, yeah," she replied. "It was common for me at my yard."

"Okay," I added. "Then you don't really know that well, and here on The Academy we don't judge people via sex or other factors, if they are pro, then they are pro."

"What kind of academy are you guys?" Sierra queered.

"An equal one and a traditional-modern one," I answered.

"God," Sierra scoffed. "You guys are weird!"

"We try not to be," I replied. "But I guess that's how we get through our days."

Awkwardly silence fell after I responded Sierra's comment. "Okay then," I shrugged. "Expect more of this from now on."

"What? The friendship?" Sierra asked.

"Uh, yes, that too," I answered slowly. "And the major incident likes the, uh, um, the one...that...happened...recently."

"Oh," Sierra nodded then shook her head. "Why?"

"Well," I explained. "I know that as a fact that, well, that psycho is still on the loose, and he might get us not now, but later on. Anyway expect something else like that to happen."

"Why?" she asked.

I looked at her; I took a deep breath. "You know this world ain't sugar coated right?" I asked.

"Uh, yeah!" she answered.

"Good, because that's relatively new to me," I chuckled.

Sierra then just chuckled, "Dork."

"Well, someone in this Academy, in this division might snap and we two are gonna pay for it either way," I stated.

"Why you have that gut feeling?" Sierra inquired.
"Uh, let's say I had that feeling at the beginning of the mess," I stated.

"Oh," She gasped. "To you the truth I did kind of too, but I thought it was a stomach ache."

"Probably the same here," I agreed.

"Why?" she asked again.

"'Cause my stomach hurts like hell now," I groaned.

"You know I like it here better than at the dump at Vegas," Sierra stated.

"Well, good," I coughed. "Then you are used to the operation here at the east division of The Academy."

I just glazed at her. "You are just bored," I observed dully.

"Oh yeah," she answered with a definite nod.

"Then let's get the hell the out of here," I suggested.

"Yeah, before I fall asleep here," Sierra responded.

"Let's go," I laughed.

We both left to the shed to get ready for our training session. Along the way I had thoughts about Sierra and I. "Hey," I sighed. "I was thinking about something."

"What?" she asked.

"What we did together, how we did it we barely met and still worked together," I said.

"Only because you dragged me into it," she chuckled.

"Adam did first," I stated. "But yeah you're right."

"We will make a great team," she stated. "As long as you become like Adam, I can only deal with one them."

I just laughed as we strolled our ways back to the room.

Chapter 15: Launch
10/9/03
09:46:28 AM

I wondered a lot about the state of the Vault, in the morning I thought I should take a look at the Vault after my incident. I went down to the observation dome and found the door I came out from when I was exiting the Vault. In the corridor I found that it changed, now there was an elevator, I climbed in to it and it descended at a fast pace to the tunnel where the Vault was located. The Vault door was retrofitted with a new touch screen panel. "Someone was generous," I whispered.

Suddenly the panel beeped and lit up. "Voice recognition activated, Welcome Mr. Loya," the computer voice beeped.

"Okay," I paused, "Very generous."

I entered the vault and it was turned into a long corridor with chrome framed porcelain tiles. At the end of the corridor was another door similar to the entrance of the old Vault. It slid open when I came close to it and I entered into a hexagonal chamber with light grey concrete walls with new pipes and lighting fixtures that were modeled after Victorian lamps. At the center was a circular bench with overhead lights. There was note on the bench, "Your new home. Dream big," I read out loud. I will. I walked around the bench and saw all the equipment from my room now here organized and cleaned. One of the bench counters lit up, it was a thick Plexiglas top with a series of light bulbs underneath illuminating anything from the underside. At the walls were more vault; there were five vaults, all of them opened. Two vaults were already filled with building supplies and machinery such like drills, electric arc welders, pneumatic guns and large vats on wheels for smelting. Apparently I'm not going to use that just now, but everything else I am. In the other vault were specialized machines, large 3D printers, molding machines and such; things I can use with the aid of the on-board computers on these machines that way I won't lose a finger or hand. Then I heard ringing, it was from a phone screen from the center bench. I walked over and touched the screen and a small ear piece popped out from the side of the screen. I placed in my ear. "Hey it's Adam," Adam called.

"Oh hey, what's up?" I asked. "How did you know I was here?"

"Where?" he asked. "I just called the number I received from an email."

"I see," I paused. "Who was it from?"

"That's what I'm doing also," Adam replied.

"Are you close to finding out?" I asked.

"Er, yeah," Adam paused. "Got it-it's from Sally."

"Really?" I asked.

Then I saw a message popped up from one of the monitors on the center bench. "Wait," I called. "I got a message from her too."

"What did she say?" Adam asked. "Where is she?"

"Hold on," I protested. "Okay, I opened it."

"Well?" Adam asked.

"Hope you like your new lab, just the beginning of your expansive playground. I hope you will create real progress on the projects that are lying beneath The Academy and keep it safe until it's time," I read out load.

"What does that mean?" Adam interrupted.

"I wasn't done reading," I paused. "I heard you made progress on those artifacts Cornelius and I gave you and with the machinery you saved from the Blue Ridge Facility. I'm well rested to know you are able to crack the cipher on the blueprints and build what was meant to be built with all these parts. A long road lies ahead, many are hunting for what you hunted, since you were the first to find them all, keep them safe in this Vault, it is crucial that no one but you and your trusted companions have their hands or access to this technology."

"That was the end?" Adam asked.

"Yeah," I sighed.

"Reply back asking where is she," Adam suggested.

"Already a step ahead of you," I replied.

I typed a message back to her asking where is she and if she could comeback. "I sent it," I reported.

"Then we'll have to wait," Adam replied.

"Not that long," I paused. "I got a message back."

"Wow," Adam gasped that was quick.

"She can't tell us," I replied.

"You mean you can't tell me?" Adam asked slyly.

"No, she wrote, I can't tell you, you have to find out," I replied.

"Wow," Adam coughed. "Okay, more mysteries, God, this place is full of them!"

"Maybe because we're not that open minded," I said. "We have to keep that in mind."

"Yeah yeah," Adam yawned.

"Hey, Adam," I called.

"Yes?" he asked.

"Can you trace the signal? I mean the message?" I asked.

"I could," perked Adam. "I'm doing it right now."

I heard Adam's fingers tapping away on his keyboard faintly over the phone. "How fast you can do this?" I asked.

"Very," Adam chuckled.

He kept typing away. I heard several disgusted sighs and muffled grunts. "Sorry I didn't have my daily dose of Mountain Dew today, the cafeteria ran out," he sighed in disbelieve.

"It's alright, take your time," I replied.

Meanwhile I was just tinkering with come coils and breadboard connectors and some clutches on the bench. I continued work on that strange power supply machine and started to hook up some connections, making a fuel reservoir connecting to the tube filled with the strange liquid and putting some regulating systems on it. "Okay I..." Adam paused, "I, I just lost her, she went off the grid, everything seemed to be gone, she erased the entire trail instantly! Wow, she's good."

"Maybe she is on the run," I said. "Well you tried."

"Yeah," Adam sighed. "We need a real break."

"Well today we have nothing going today, so what do you want to do?" I asked.

"Fresh air away from here," Adam laughed. "I need to unwind somewhere far from where all this occurred!"

"We can join the field trippers to the Washington Mall," I said. "You know act like a tourist and stuff."

"That sounds fun," Adam chuckled. "I'll tell the rest of the guys, when does the bus leave?"

"It's rapid rail," I replied. "We are boarding a train from the Academy, so no need for special things, just bring a camera, some spare change for street vendors, we'll be back in time."

"Great," Adam sighed. "More trains."

"Hey, it's free, unless you want to pay for a plane ticket for all of us, round trip," I suggested.

"Yeah, no," Adam declined. "I'm good, a free ride sounds better."

"You can thank the Academy," I smiled.

"Well I'd rather have the Academy tell me what this Mickey Mouse business is all about," Adam replied.

"Me too," I paused well I'll meet you guys at platform 18, that's where the train is at, everyone meet there ten till five so we have time to find a good seat."

"Will do," Adam replied. "See you then."

He hung up and I stared at the screen. Then I began to type another message to Sally. “Did you meet Cornelius in person?” I whispered.

A message came back instantly, “No.”

“How did he contact you then?” I asked while I typed it.

A message came back. “Same way I’m doing with you,” I read aloud.

I sighed and looked at the screen and rocked back and forth just a little bit. “Okay, Cornelius should be trusted, he knows what he is doing, I hope,” I sighed.

I walked towards the main entrance and the lights shut off, all the equipment powered down. And I walked down the corridor entrance, the door behind me shut with a complex arrangement of clicking and thumping as the tumblers of the lock were rearranged. The large vault door ahead opened and as I walked by it the door began to roll shut heavily. I climbed to the elevator and began my climb to the top. I got out of the elevator and out to the Observation Dome, then I took the tram down to the station to meet up with the guys.

It was almost ten ‘til five when I entered the station and headed my way through the crowds to platform 18, walking on the bridge that spans over the tops of the trains below. I found them waiting around, Sierra was just walking towards Adam and Devon, and both of them were waiting besides the lamppost. “Hey look its Sierra!” Adam yelled.

“Bryan is just at the stairs,” Devon called.

“What’s up?” I asked. “Let’s get into the train, it’s leaving soon.”

Adam, Devon, Sierra and I climbed into the luxurious train. We found our seats reserved in the Pullman car. The luxurious brown-reddish leather seats felt very comfortable. Adam, Devon and Scotty sat in the seat in front of Sierra and I. I had the window seat when Sierra was in the middle seat and no one had the aisle. The train jerked forward, we could hear the loud chattering of the passengers outside being muffled by the announcement in the train. “Next stop, Washington Union Station.” the P.A. system was turned off as the train took another jerk forward. The crowd scene of the station was being replaced by the scene of the city of Roanoke. The train rattled along the steel rails as the train picked up speed when it reached the station limit. We could see the Manor from the cut through the rocky hills. Soon we passed the old signal tower at the edge of the yard as we began to cross the bridge. As I was enjoying the rainy but yet beautiful Virginian scene, Sierra turned her seat into a recliner. “Finally,” she moaned, “A real day-off.”

That was the truth folks. For once I have a relaxing; trouble-free day-off from the bee-hive I called the railroad. Escaping from the towering steel towers, white-hot steam from the pistons and the loud clanging of the freight trains streaming down the two silver rails that stretch across to every place you could imagine on land, from the busy growing city of Roanoke to the relaxing Roanoke Valley and the graceful Shenandoah Valley. The rain wasn't all that bad, it wasn't pouring down like there was no tomorrow, but it was light and soothing. The autumn trees were soaked in the small droplets of water from the light gray clouds. The train was now really picking up speed as it started to climb the Blue Ridge Mountains and head down the grade into the Virginian plains. As the enterprising scene sink into my mind, I began thinking about the days when the railroads were at full swing. When people traveled on the rails to go to distant places from their home, times when the passenger trains were there to comfort passengers on their ride to towns, cities new and old. The times, the era when riding the railroad means going on an epic adventure of relaxation and exploration. When the long luxury trains were a way for people to really kick off and enjoy their ride to their destination, and with regular passenger trains, they to have their own luxury, the luxury of adventure and imagination to anyone of any age. Riding the rails from a city towering with dizzying and beautiful skyscrapers to a the lovely country side where trees are flourishing in green and into the flat plains of the Midwest where you could see an ocean of wheat waving it the wind as the train rumble pass by and up the ridged mountains of the Rockies, twisting and turning with the tracks that weave their way through the mountains. Then down into the deserts of the southwest experiencing the scenery of cactus and coyotes chasing the trains as it glides over the desert ground and through warm climates of southern California. Or to any place we could even imagine to go to. I mean on small trip on a train from one town to another with any amount of miles in between your two destinations, you are going to experience railroading and see things at a different point of view, psychologically and physically. I mean to me, something that is moving at a hundred miles an hour is not fast unless that machine is about four hundred tons and hauling at least a thousand ton or eight hundred tons up a mountainous grade. That's the beauty of railroads, their history and efficiency that built a network to link a country in one harmonious tune.

When I turned my head to talk to Sierra, she was sleeping; then again I don't blame her. We were on the train for at least an hour and we are starting to head into the plains. This is sure relaxing, no wonder she wanted to ride it for a long time, well since she entered the company that is. In front Devon and Scotty was playing Rock, Paper, Scissors, Slap. Their hands were red as the fire in the firebox of *Black Bullet*. Adam was playing a game on his cell phone with his head against the window. He was about to fall asleep on the seat across the aisle. I lay down on my seat and kicked back as the soft sound of the clickety-clack of the wheels rolling on the rails was drowned from the gentle tapping of the rain on the window. I fell asleep knowing that things finally cooled down enough enjoy what life has to offer.

For some hours and minutes I was asleep until the announcements woke me up. "Washington Union Station," the announcement mumbled.

"Bryan! Bryan!" Sierra exclaimed.

"Huh, wha?" I yawned.

"You fell asleep," Sierra stated. "We are here."

"God!" I gasped. "The trip was that short?"

"No," Sierra prompted. "We had to slow down because of the wet rails in Culpeper."

"Okay," I grunted as I got up from the leather seat. "Next we are going shopping."

"Good," Sierra smiled. "I need new boots and clothes."

"Alright," I replied. "To the mall then."

Sierra and I woke up the rest of the crew who was snoring and drooling on the seats. "Guys, up!" I exclaimed. "We are in Washington already."

"Uh, give me another hour," Adam droned.

"We are in a train stupid," Sierra declared.

When Sierra was pulling Adam out of his seat, I saw someone strange out in the platform. It was a tall man in a black hat and suit. He had a yellow walkie-talkie in his hand and seemed to be talking to someone. On the other side was Jefferson with her cell phone. She too was talking to someone. I was stood there frozen. Is it possible, is she really? Sierra finally pulled Adam off the seat, and stared at me with curiosity.

"Bryan," she called. "Is something wrong?"

"Soon," I answered worried. "Very soon.

Epilogue
10/10/03
12:21:00 PM

I don't know; this entire thing was off the wall compared to my year before this incident. But now I know more about the Academy then anytime before. With Sally contacting me once in a while to give me more reports and clues, I'm just well on my way of figuring out the entire mystery. Cornelius hasn't spoken to me, despite the fact that I'm using his chamber as my lab now. It was remodeled to be like the lab in the Blue Ridge Facility, hexagonal but much cleaner. Someone did remodel it for me and was very generous with the design and equipment that was placed here. But as I worked down here on my spare time, I was deciphering the code on the blueprints, now that I have all of it deciphered I noted the wording was weird too, some sort of code, well I think it its some sort of code. The center of some of these projects were all the same component, a very complex one to build and to understand but it was labeled The Heart, and it had the same cores that the center of the mysterious power supply had. "What could this be?" I asked myself.

Hours went by as I tried to figure out why this was called The Heart. The components to make up the entire machine were similar to the one as the power supply, but this one was a variable input and output machine. The mysterious power supply had a fixed input and output frequency, this machine dubbed "The Heart", "The Core" by me was a variable machine, so complex but the function was mysterious but simple by my guessing. Some of the information I do not understand, but I guess if I'm at it I might understand what goes where and why. With that in mind, it might take me years to figure this one out, but I have all the time until I graduate when I'm 18. That's plenty of time,

I hope. But who knows that events might occur between now and then. They might accelerate or stall my progress on this machine. I'm so transfixed on this machine because it seems to be a combination of every central component in all the projects I uncovered from the Data drive and blueprints from the Blue Ridge Facility. That's why I called it "The Core". "This is all so strange," I kept laughing to myself.

"Whoever created you," I said to the unfinished component of the machine, "was smart. Very, very smart and very elegant in the design, I might add."

Whoever created all this, was an artist at hand, these designs were from a fluent creative mind of an artist with the discipline of a rigid engineer. It'll be too much to call this person a god, just a super genius. I'll be surprised if it was a kid like me, they will be like that short cartoon kid with glasses, Dexter or the one with the funny hair, Jimmy on that new show on T.V. Maybe this project will progress along ways with me, since I have an agile mind, maybe the person who created and hid this wanted a kid like me to find it and move on with it, since that person couldn't anymore. I wonder what happened then. Who knows, any guess is as good as mine. Whatever reason it may be, it's my turn with these gadgets. Probably the only turn left, who knows, the foundation seemed to be set; it's up to me now. Like a search or a hunt to figure out what this hexagon can do.

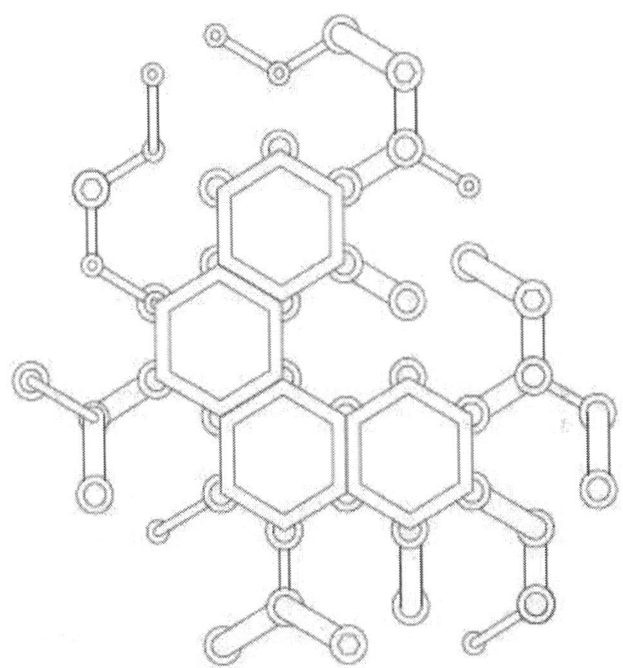

Additional Entry
Archive Footage 1.1.1

.../ArLiRep/Archive_1/Footage_1_1_1.avi
/downloading_footage...
/streaming_error_
/rerouting...
/downloading_transcript...
/transcript_loaded
Location: Blocked | Timestamp/Date: October 12, 2003 12:35:22 P.M.

(Two men standing in front of a large monitor, a panel was glowing with banks of servers beneath with lights flickering away. One of the men, tall facing the monitor stood like a statue, chewing on a toothpick.)

Tall Man: What do you want Agent 30?

Agent 30: The student knows more than he's supposed to.

Tall Man: Did he disrupt the program?

Agent 30: Well, he did stop an unauthorized-

Tall Man: Has the program been disrupted?

Agent 30: No, in fact he protected it.

Tall Man: That's all I needed to know.

Agent 30: But what if he find out too early?

Tall Man: He won't, besides he'll know when will be the right time to unravel all this. Remember we spent decades designing this program. His will won't let him arrive at the conclusion too early. You worry too much Agent 30.

Agent 30: He's extremely talented and bright-

Tall Man: He's far smarter than any student previously in this academy. I know I read the reports.

Agent 30: Can he engineer The Hive back into order?

Tall Man: I don't think that's the right question to ponder about. The correct and more informative one would be, could he build it better? What can he build from that seed project?

Agent 30: Right.

(Agent 30 turns around about to head to the door. The Tall Man turns around)

(Camera Two: Light from the monitor illuminates the back of the Tall Man, shows the back wall of the room, Agent 30 at the doorway.)

Tall Man: Agent 30, send in Order 10.

Agent 30: But we are in the middle of constructing the last of the system, you want us to back off?

Tall Man: Remember we will monitor and help when it's needed. The help will just be to repair parts of the system that has been damaged in any event.

Agent 30: You know we will die.

Tall Man: Then you signed up for the wrong job. I warn you do not interfere, or you'll guarantee your own death.

Agent 30: Order 10 it is.

Tall Man: Yes (Pauses) Execute Order 10, and do not put a finger on them. This bugger bites.

<End of Transcript>

/About The Author/

Bryan Loya is an independent writer, been writing stories since the 6th grade and ever since been building up a world of technology, mystery and one of kind characters. He is currently a student at New Mexico State University in Las Cruces, New Mexico studying in Civil Engineering. The Hunt is his first publication, in many in a long line of future books in the series. He currently resides in New Mexico.

//Follow the Author
Twitter @bryloya
Instagram @bryarchitect

\\\Like us on Facebook!
www.facebook.com/OldDominionJournals

\\\Follow us on Twitter!
@OldDominJournal

\\\Follow the blog!
Bryarchitect.wordpress.com

Made in the USA
San Bernardino, CA
13 August 2016